HOUSE OF RED

ELI SICKLER

**HELLBENDER
BOOKS**

an imprint of Sunbury Press, Inc.
Mechanicsburg, PA USA

an imprint of Sunbury Press, Inc.
Mechanicsburg, PA USA

For information about special discounts for bulk purchases, please contact Sunbury Press Orders Dept. at (855) 338-8359 or orders@sunburypress.com.

To request one of our authors for speaking engagements or book signings, please contact Sunbury Press Publicity Dept. at publicity@sunburypress.com.

FIRST HELLBENDER BOOKS EDITION: October 2023

Set in Adobe Garamond | Interior design by Crystal Devine | Cover by Igor Andric | Edited by Lawrence Knorr.

Publisher's Cataloging-in-Publication Data
Names: Sickler, Elizabeth, author.
Title: House of Red / Elizabeth Sickler.
Description: First Trade paperback edition. | Mechanicsburg, PA : Hellbender Books, 2023.
Summary: Once upon a time . . . we all know the classic stories of Little Red Riding Hood, Snow White and Hansel and Gretel. Now read about what really happened to Red, Snow and the Witch in this fantasy re-telling involving werewolves, magic and a Huntsman who is not what he seems.
Identifiers: ISBN : 979-8-88819-164-4 (softcover) | ISBN : 979-8-88819-165-1 (ePub).
Subjects: FICTION / Fantasy / Action & Adventure | YOUNG ADULT FICTION / Animals / Mythical Creatures | YOUNG ADULT FICTION / Fairy Tales & Folklore / General.

Product of the United States of America
0 1 1 2 3 5 8 13 21 34 55

Continue the Enlightenment!

For Grandma

PROLOGUE

Autumn was a liminal time, a time of change when the wind began to shift from hot summer breezes to chilly winter squalls. The trees were beginning their transition to hibernation, with their dying leaf smell filling the air.

Vivie turned her face towards the breeze and inhaled deeply. She loved the crisp smell of autumn, of the loamy scent of the woods with the promise of apples to come. She opened her eyes and turned to look back towards the farm.

She couldn't see it, of course, since she was all the way out in the northeast corner of her family's fields. She couldn't even see the cottage's smoke from the chimney all the way out here. She was out beyond the last small hill, near the cornerstone that separated the farm's property from the forest.

The boulder itself was set back from the forest a bit, and there was a narrow berm between it and the start of the tree line. Vivie loved it here because of the dichotomy of the gently tamed fields next to the wild greenwood.

She began to dance around the large rock, giggling with delight. Her parents didn't like her being so close to the woods, but she enjoyed the delicate balance she felt between what was safe and familiar and the primitive call of the deep forest.

She bowed to her stoic stone partner, giggled again, and then skipped back through the long grass towards home.

Vivie spread her hands wide, closed her eyes, and started spinning in a circle, soaking up the sunshine.

The sun was still out longer than the moon, and its waning warmth was welcome, even after the summer heat.

With winter beginning to creep across the land and the last few days of harvest coming on, Vivie and her family would soon be busy making final preparations for the cold season.

But here and today, she could enjoy herself.

She began to spin faster, her long honey-colored braid flaring out around her. When she was sufficiently dizzy and had to struggle to keep her balance, she flopped down into the grass and sighed happily.

Suddenly, an eerie howl split the pleasant afternoon birdsong and cricket chirps.

Vivie snapped to attention, sitting up and looking around wide-eyed. It was suddenly absolutely quiet; no small animal or insect noises and no breeze rustling the trees.

She held her breath and waited, looking nervously towards the tree line. She gathered her feet under herself, ready to run at the first sight of danger.

Her hazel eyes scanned the area, but she didn't see any immediate threat. She glanced towards the sun; she had been taught from an early age that she didn't want to be caught anywhere near the woods close to sundown. The sun was still high enough in the sky that she had plenty of daylight left.

Vivie looked towards the forest again but still didn't see anything. She squinted at the cornerstone as if it held the answer, but it was as grey and impassive as ever. She waited to see if she heard the strange howl again. It wasn't like wolves to hunt with the sun still out, as they likely wouldn't find any prey.

After several more moments of remaining motionless, she heard birds start singing again, and a grasshopper jumped near her. She caught the movement out of the corner of her eye and flinched with fright.

Blowing out her breath, she shook her head at her foolishness; there was nothing to be afraid of, and she must have imagined the peculiar howl since daydreaming out here was one of her favorite pastimes.

"I should be more like you, old rock; serious, solid and unmoving." She looked at the boulder and smirked. "But I don't think I look as nice in shades of grey."

She relaxed her tensed muscles and laid back down in the grass. With the tall grass around her, she gazed at the fluffy clouds overhead, imagining they were pretty bunnies frolicking with dapper frog gentlemen. The blue sky was bright, and with the sun shining, it made her think of fancy icing on a sweet apple cake.

She yawned and lazily closed her eyes, soaking up the sun.

She was just about to drift off to a lovely nap when she heard the howl again. This time, it sounded closer.

Vivie lurched to her feet, grass clinging to her hair as she looked around wildly. Another howl began before the final echoes of the first had completely died away. The sound created a sort of spooky melody that raised the hairs on Vivie's arms and the back of her neck.

Her eyes snapped towards the edge of the forest. Within the cover of the trees, it was dark, even with the sun still shining overhead. It looked gloomy, and she had to suppress a shudder.

The lone howl came again, high and otherworldly, and she was just about to start hurrying back home when a huge black wolf stepped out of the tree line. She froze at the sight of the beast as it came towards her across the berm, and she began to tremble in fear.

The wolf in front of her howled again, but this time, it was low and mournful-sounding rather than the piercing high hunting call it had used earlier. The sound caused Vivie's eyes to widen, and she rubbed her hands over her arms to try to stop shaking.

The wolf came closer. It didn't seem fearful of a human at all. Its eyes were a curious shade of pale grey, almost silver-colored, and they stayed locked with Vivie's own as it approached. As it moved, the sunlight reflected in those shining, silvery eyes, and it reminded Vivie of the full moon on a cloudless night.

Seeing this large wolf alone and leaving the safety of the forest was odd. Something about this creature, with its abnormal size and clear, level gaze seemingly directed at her, was unnerving. It felt as if the wolf were looking through her rather than at her.

Vivie took a deep breath and was just about to run when the wolf unexpectedly stopped walking towards her. She blinked in surprise; she had been expecting it to continue towards her.

She clenched her fists with resolve and then took a halting step backward, away from the beast. Then she took another. However, as she lifted her foot to take a third step, the wolf advanced again in two quick steps, mimicking her moments. She stepped sideways to her right and chanced a glance towards where she knew home and safety were. The wolf did the same; a step to the right, and then it stopped and stood motionless.

She looked to her left, where the boulder sat, and wondered how fast she would have to be to reach it and higher ground before the wolf could get to her. The large rock was only a few paces away.

Trying to keep the wolf in sight, she took another step sideways, this time to her left. The movement put her one step closer to the boulder and potential safety, but the wolf again imitated her.

She stood frozen in both awe and terror, with the beast within an easy bound of her.

Vivie gulped and glanced again towards the rock. Steeling herself, she lunged towards the boulder as fast as she could. Her hands grasped the cool stone, and she was about to start scrambling up it when she felt the hot breath of the wolf on the back of her neck.

She braced herself, expecting the wolf to tear into her, when suddenly a shot rang out across the deadly quiet air.

Vivie scrunched her eyes shut tight and held her breath, clinging to the boulder for support.

There was a dull thud behind her, and she slowly opened her eyes and looked towards the source of the sound.

It looked as if the wolf had taken one more halting step forward and had then collapsed in a heap at her feet. It was just behind her, and she nudged its nose with her foot. It didn't move or even twitch.

Unexpectedly, Vivie's eyes welled with tears. She raised her eyes from the ground and looked for the source of the gunshot. Her gaze landed on a tall, muscular young man standing on the hillside behind her. He lowered his smoking gun and tipped his large black furry hat towards her.

A huntsman had rescued her just in time.

Vivie stepped around the slain wolf and eyed her would-be champion. He was smiling broadly as he walked towards her, but on his weathered face, it looked more like a grimace, as if he wasn't used to smiling.

He waited, a cocky smile on his lips as if he expected her to gush about how grateful she was for him saving her life from the slavering monster now lying dead behind her.

Vivie found that his self-assured manner did not make her feel safer, but rather, his arrogant attitude made her feel as if there was something else lurking behind his beady black eyes.

After a few moments of awkward silence between them, Vivie looked at her feet and then dipped her head. "Thank you, sir, for saving my life."

He nodded once and then reached for her arm. She let him do so, knowing that he meant to escort her home after her ordeal.

He turned her back towards her cottage and, with a firm hand on her arm, guided her in that direction.

She let him keep his hand there for a few paces and then tried to pull her arm away from him discreetly; she was perfectly capable of walking home, even after her fright. At the slight movement of her arm, though, his hand clenched down tighter, and she had to suppress a sudden yelp. His grip wasn't painful yet, but she suspected that this man of the woods could become a dangerous enemy if he were angered.

She glanced at him, but his eyes were focused intently ahead of them, almost as if he could guess what she was thinking, and he was dutifully ignoring her. She thought she saw the corner of his mouth twitch in a slight smug smile.

Vivie shook her head and realized she must be in shock and recovering from her fear. She let him continue to guide her home.

Later that night, once she was safely tucked in her own bed and as she was trying to fall asleep, Vivie swore she could still feel the huntsman's controlling grip on her arm. She hoped she would never need his services again because something about him made her feel wary and like she wanted to run as far away from him as she could. He seemed more dangerous than the wild wolf had been.

Vivie sighed and pushed that thought from her mind. *Wolves were more dangerous than a huntsman . . . weren't they?*

ONE

Once upon a time, there was a little girl who lived on the edge of the forest. She lived with her mother and father and often ventured into the woods to visit her grandmother. When not walking through the woods alone, she could be found wandering in the fields near her parents' cottage.

Her father was a simple farmer, so he took care of the fields around their home. He worked long hours and would often not come in for dinner until well into the evening.

Their home was not fancy; the walls were made of simple wood and were merely whitewashed rather than painted. The floor was covered in rushes that were often in need of changing. Yet the entire home was clean and tidy, with everything in its proper place. They did not have a lot of money, but despite this, they were all happy and content.

On one bright and sunny morning in the middle of September, the young girl's mother was sweeping the floors, as usual. The harvest was almost over, and the leaves had begun to fall from the trees, so she was trying, in vain, to keep more dirt from entering the already dirty house. It was after breakfast, and the girl's father had already left to work the last of the fields, bringing in hay and some of the last remaining vegetables before the first frosts of fall. They had to pay a debt to a local landowner but could also keep enough to feed themselves throughout the long and cold winter.

As it was nearing lunchtime, the young girl's mother called out to her daughter, "Vivie! Come in, child; we will be having lunch shortly. Your father is on his way in from the fields and will be joining us."

Vivie, who had been sitting out in the garden reading a book, glanced up and nodded at her mother. She stood up slowly and stretched, reaching her hands up to the blue sky and smiling broadly. Her petite frame had some muscle on it from a life of labor despite her tender age of seventeen. She felt her muscles stretch and thought that it felt good to be alive!

Not for the first time that day, she glanced toward the bright blue sky. *I wonder what is out there in the world.* She thought. She glanced towards the cottage and sighed. *Is this all I have to look forward to?* Then she glanced at her book, laying open on the garden wall. *What if there's more out there?*

Her thoughts were cut short as her mother called for her again, "Vivie Madalla, stop dawdling and come inside to help me with lunch!"

Vivie flicked her long, honey-colored braid over her shoulder and walked towards the cottage. As she approached the doorway, their eyes met, and her mother's hazel eyes smiled to match Vivie's own. "Please prepare lunch for us. You know your father will want to get back out to work as soon as he's finished. He doesn't like to be kept waiting."

Vivie nodded and went inside to make lunch. It was a simple fair: crusty bread with some cheese from their one and only cow. Even though it was getting late in the season, they still had a few apples left, so she added those to a plate as well. Finally, she went out back to their water pump and filled a pitcher with cold, clear water.

Almost as soon as she had finished setting their small table, they heard boots outside coming up the walk. Vivie walked to the door and stood beside her mother as they greeted her father.

He was tall and thin and always looked worn and tired from a lifetime of hard labor outside. His skin was naturally tanned from long hours spent in the sun, and his hands, though large and strong, had callouses from working all of his life.

First, he greeted his wife with a soft kiss on her cheek. He may have been a simple farmer, but he always treated Vivie's mother with love and respect. At the kiss, she blushed like a schoolgirl and giggled. She wiped her hands on her apron and then moved aside to let him into their home.

As he entered the room, he turned to Vivie and patted her shoulder. "I see you've made us a fine lunch again."

"Oh Papa, you know we always have the same thing. It's not much, but it tastes good." She replied.

He nodded and took a seat. Both Vivie and her mother joined him at the table. After a small prayer thanking the Creator for their meager fare, they dug in.

As Vivie bit into a slice of her apple, her mind wandered back to her earlier thoughts. *Is this all there is?* True, the apple was juicy, but was this all she had to look forward to as she grew older? She looked out their door. *Could a different life than farming be out there for me?*

They finished the small meal in silence, and once they were finished, Papa rose and strode towards the door to return to work. As he reached the door, he brushed his hand over the old double-barrel shotgun resting beside it. It was tradition, as the weapon had been in the family for generations. As it was so old, an antique, he briefly wondered if it would even shoot anymore. He then turned and nodded once as if coming to a decision. He came back to Mama, kissed her on the cheek and then turned to Vivie. "I think you should take some food to Grandma today. It's been a while since anyone visited her, and I worry about the old woman living alone deep in the forest."

Vivie smiled; she enjoyed visiting her grandmother. And an afternoon walk through the forest would be pleasant in autumn. "Aye, Papa. I'll prepare a basket and then take it to her."

Her mother nodded, "That is an excellent idea, but please be careful. And you must be home before dark."

"I will, Mama."

She then grabbed a basket and began placing simple items inside it. She took a fresh loaf of bread that Mama had baked only yesterday, a few wedges of cheese (cheddar, Grandma's favorite) and a small slab of dried beef. Then, as a surprise, she put in a few cookies they had been saving for Sunday dinner. Grandma loved to bake, but in her old age, and because she lived alone, she rarely did it anymore. Cookies would make her smile.

Once the basket was ready, Vivie was about to leave when her mother caught her arm in the doorway. "Aren't you forgetting something?"

Vivie furrowed her eyebrows. "I have the food and myself, so no? What else am I forgetting?"

Her mother smiled and went back into the cottage. She came back with a bundle in her arms, which she shook out before handing it to Vivie. "I know it's not too cold outside yet, but this will keep you warm, dry and comfortable." She held out a red woolen cloak to her daughter.

The girl smiled and put the basket down to tie the long cloak around her slender shoulders. She adjusted the tie, and then her mother reached forward and settled the deep hood in place. "Now you're all set."

Vivie nodded and kissed her mother's cheek. "I promise to be back before dark, Mama."

"See that you are; there are dangerous things that lurk in the forest after dark."

And with that, Vivie began to make her way to her grandmother's house.

Two

It was getting into the late afternoon, so the light was good. As she entered the forest, Vivie could still see her mother standing in the doorway of their small cottage, watching her. She turned and waved once before following the path into the trees. She knew her mother would watch her until she was out of sight, and she couldn't help but roll her eyes at her mother's apparent concern. She was just going to Grandma's house, something she did fairly often; she would be fine. Besides, she wasn't a child anymore; she could take care of herself now.

As soon as she stepped into the woods, the light became dimmer as the tree branches blocked the sun. Vivie was still able to see where she was going, though, and her hazel eyes soon adjusted to the gloom. As she walked along, she inhaled deeply, and the crisp scent of dead leaves and freshly turned earth greeted her. She smiled and then skipped a few paces.

After a few moments, she stopped skipping and just took in the sights and sounds around her. The trees were thick here already, even though she had not walked far into the forest. They were mostly pine trees, and their soft needles littered the ground along the path, which made her footsteps fall softly, barely making a sound. A bird's song reached her ears, and she looked skywards toward the sound.

Vivie continued to walk, and the farther into the woods she walked, the thicker the trees became. She was now walking amongst strong oak and maple trees, their large branches creaking gently in a mild breeze. Here, the trees were ancient and almost completely blocked out the sun.

Despite this, there were late-blooming flowers scattered here and there among the undergrowth. She caught a glimpse of tiny, white, star-shaped flowers nestled among bolder, blue ones. *Perhaps I could move to the village and become a seamstress. All these pretty flowers would inspire me to sew beautiful dresses.* She thought as she walked.

She kept to the path. While it was tempting to wander off in search of that bird singing or to pick a bouquet for Grandma, Vivie kept her worn brown shoes strictly on the path. You never knew what was lurking in the dark undergrowth.

After almost an hour of just walking through the forest and enjoying the serenity, she heard off in the distance a wolf howling. It was long and mournful and sounded sad, but it was also eerie in the darkening gloom, so Vivie began to hurry her footsteps. On a normal trip to Grandma's house, it would take her no more than two hours, so long as she didn't stop to admire a tree or listen to a babbling brook, but something about the howling was ethereal and unnerving, even though she had heard wolves howling plenty of times before, so she hurried towards Grandma's house and finally rounded the last turn in the path that would bring her into sight of the cottage.

She approached the door and walked up the three small stone steps, then rang the little bell. There was a shuffling sound from within, and a few moments later, the door opened to reveal an old woman with curly grey hair that was covered by a mop cap. She had glasses perched on her nose, and kindly-looking blue eyes peered out through them. As soon as her eyes recognized Vivie, her entire face lit up into a broad smile. "Vivie! What a pleasant surprise! Come in, child!"

As Vivie entered the small cottage, she was greeted by a warm interior. The hearth was going with a roaring fire, and there was a small kettle hanging over it. There was plush furniture everywhere, including an over-stuffed chair, which Grandma walked over to and sat down in. She promptly picked up a small basket and began to work on her knitting, which she had just set aside when she had answered the door.

Vivie walked over to the small kitchen and placed the basket on the counter. She then removed her red cloak, which Grandma eyed dubiously, before beginning to put away the food she had brought with her.

"Would you like me to prepare you some supper before I leave Grandma?"

"That would be nice, dear. Just a small fare is fine. Won't you be joining me?"

"I can stay for a little while, but Mama said to be home before full dark."

Grandma pondered that for a moment and then nodded. "She's right; there are dark things out in that forest."

Vivie turned to look quizzically at her. "I thought the tales of monsters were just to scare little children into behaving."

Grandma shook her head, and some of her curls jiggled. "Oh no, dear, there are real dangers out there."

Vivie shrugged. The world was much larger than she was familiar with. But that didn't mean she believed in fairy stories told around a campfire. "All the same, I promised I'd be home tonight." Privately, she thought, *I'm old enough now not to be scared by children's monsters.*

Grandma nodded and then put away her knitting needles. She came over to stand beside Vivie and ran her withered hands through the girl's long plait fondly. Then she eyed the red cloak again.

"Why do you dislike my cloak so much? You made it, after all." Vivie said as she began slicing some cheese.

The old woman shrugged. "When I made it, I thought the color would fade a bit over time. It's so garish and too bright. Why, the man in the moon could see you out and about at night in that thing!"

Vivie chuckled. "But this way, Mama can see me as I come home. As soon as I leave the forest, she can catch sight of my red cloak and know I'm on my way."

Grandma's tone turned serious. "All true, but then, so can other things."

Vivie furrowed her eyebrows. "What is out there, waiting in the woods?"

There was a long silence, and finally, Vivie turned to face her Grandma. The old woman sighed and walked back towards her plush chair. "A girl of your age, at only seventeen, does not know much of this world." She sat down again, resting her old bones. "There are . . . things out there, Vivie." The old woman closed her eyes and shuddered slightly.

As she did so, Vivie rolled her eyes. *Why is everyone so concerned for my safety? I can take care of myself.*

"Things that would turn your blood to ice and make your skin crawl. Things that come scratching at your door at night . . ."

No sooner had she uttered those chilling words, but there came a light scratching at the cottage door. It was so faint that Vivie thought at first she had imagined it. When the sound did not repeat itself, she rolled her eyes; it must just be her imagination since Grandma was good at telling scary stories. After the sounds of the forest and this warning, Vivie was beginning to feel slightly nervous.

She turned around to look at Grandma to see if she had heard the noise, too or if she was trying to frighten her. But Grandma's eyes were locked on the door, a strange expression on her withered old face.

Vivie felt her gaze shift there, almost involuntarily, and she held her breath, waiting to hear if the sound came again. Moments passed, and nothing happened. She shook her head and went back to preparing dinner. She had just gotten to the point of convincing herself that it had all been the wind when there it was again: a light scratching sound, as if from a branch, scraping against the door to Grandma's house. Her eyes snapped to Grandma, who was now white as a sheet. The old woman stood up slowly and placed a gnarled finger to her lips for silence. Very slowly, she cautiously made her way to the door. The latch was, thankfully, closed.

However, when she was within a few steps from the door, there came a very low, almost inaudible, growling sound. Vivie felt her eyes widen in panic. Had that been in her imagination?

But again, there came the growling sound, even as Grandma hastily backed away from the door. Her eyes snapped to Vivie's, and she motioned for her to join her back towards the small bedroom. Vivie shuffled across the floor, trying to be as quiet as she could but feeling as if her small feet were stomping across the floor.

They had reached the doorway to the bedroom when the soft scratching turned into frenzied clawing. Vivie could easily picture the outside of the door being shredded beneath the inch-long talons of some indescribably fearsome beast. She shuddered and hugged Grandma tight. The two of them stood motionless together, clinging to the other in fear. Vivie heard the timbers of the door begin to creak and groan. The scrabbling intensified, and the door creaked more. At any moment, whatever was on the outside of the door would be inside with them.

Grandma seemed to shudder involuntarily as if snapping herself out of her fright, and then she pushed Vivie towards the other side of her bed. She slammed the bedroom door shut and threw the bolt home. Then she came around to her bed and reached under it. She removed a long leather case, and when she opened it, Vivie caught sight of a gleaming silver barreled shotgun. Grandma was not going to go down without a fight.

"Where did you . . . ?" Vivie began.

Grandma shook her head as she loaded the weapon with bullets. They glowed shiny in the candlelight, which illuminated the little room with flickering movement. "Best not to talk, dear, just stay behind me. If that beast gets through, I'm going to give it what for!" She leveled the gun towards the door of her bedroom and took a few steadying breaths. Then she calmly waited, her stance and demeanor wary and alert.

Vivie realized, in a detached sort of way, that she should be concerned about *why* Grandma had a gun and knew how to use it. She shook those thoughts away and again focused on the seemingly thin piece of wood separating them from a rampaging monster.

Again, they could hear the timbers of the front door rattling in its hinges as grunts and growling accompanied it. Then, with a resounding shock that Vivie felt all the way through her toes, the front door fell inwards in a great boom that shook the rest of the house.

She didn't know what to expect next, but it certainly wasn't silence. Not a sound came from the front room after she imagined the dust settling from the crashing door. Not even animal sounds from whatever was out there. Vivie craned her ears for the slightest sound of footsteps or breathing but heard nothing. She looked at Grandma in confusion: had the thing, by some remote, lucky chance, gone away?

Grandma's gaze remained locked on the bedroom door.

Vivie was just about to breathe a sigh of relief, thinking that perhaps this was nothing more than a bad dream and she was at home, lying on her small pallet on the floor with her parents sleeping nearby, when there came a great, wet snuffling sound beneath the bedroom door.

Vivie's eyes snapped to the bottom of the door, and she imagined she could see a large, black nose, not unlike her neighbor's sheepdog's nose, sniffing and snorting from the other side.

She began to shake with fear. Grandma took a deep breath and widened her stance, holding the gun at the ready.

Again, the sound of raking claws and groaning wood was heard. Vivie imagined that she could actually see the wood bending inwards, fragile as a spider's web, about to break. She squeezed her eyes shut and knelt on the floor on the other side of Grandma's bed.

She clutched at her red cloak. Her eyes suddenly snapped open: how was she still wearing that? Hadn't she taken it off just after arriving? She put a hand to her forehead; this must surely be a dream. The claws ripped at the door again, this time growing more frenzied, and Vivie shook her head; a nightmare and not a dream.

She clenched and unclenched the cloak in her hands and could not bring herself to let go of the bright red fabric. She realized that in their haste to retreat to the bedroom and, hopefully, safety, she must have instinctively reached out for the garment. Its soft texture and comforting warmth offered her a small semblance of peace, and she thought that if she survived this encounter, she would never take the cloak off again.

As the sound of rasping claws continued, the noises the beast was making increased as well until there was a loud, keening wail coming from the other side of the door. Vivie realized that it sounded similar, although not identical, to the wolf howl she had heard earlier in the forest. She wondered, in a detached sort of fashion, if it was the same animal making these noises now. Then she shook her head as she realized that wolves did not simply break down people's doors. This creature, whatever it was, was mad in anger and intent only on destruction. Wolves, and all wild animals for that matter, rarely attacked humans. And never in something as ruthless as anger. That was a human trait.

The door creaked and groaned again until suddenly, in a shower of wood chips and splinters, it simply burst apart. As the dust settled, Vivie finally caught sight of what was on the other side of the door as she poked her head out around the side of the bed.

It was a huge wolf, almost as large as a pony, with glossy black fur that glinted in the candlelight. Its fur also stuck up at odd angles, giving it a strange, haloed appearance. Its paws were easily the size of dinner plates, and its long tail lashed behind it in an agitated fashion, back and forth.

Now that the door was down, the beast stared into the room, its gaze sweeping back and forth as if looking for something in particular. Vivie realized then that this was no normal wolf, not even simply a large one of its species. This was a monster from the deepest recesses of the forest, a creature that, only a moment before, or so it seemed, Grandma had been warning her about.

The beast's gaze landed on Vivie, and she shrank back from it, holding up her red cloak as if the flimsy material could shield her from the monster. The creature's eyes locked onto her, and she saw they were a hellish fiery red color, matched by her cloak. Its eyes smoldered with rage, and it took one slow step forward into the room.

The sound of a hammer clicking back echoed throughout the deadly quiet room.

The beast's eyes snapped toward the sound, and the eyes narrowed in warning. A low, deep growl bubbled out of its throat, and it took another, albeit more tentative, step forward.

"Best not test my patience anymore, beasty. Those doors will already cost me a fortune." Grandma snarled.

Vivie was taken aback; she had never once, in all her life, heard her grandmother utter a word of anger or disapproval towards anyone. Now, here she was, talking to a monster about something as simple as replacing a door. She sounded so calm and matter-of-fact about it, too.

The wolf growled again, and Vivie felt sure she could feel the timbers in the wall shaking, too. She felt its rumbling echo throughout her chest as she took a gasping breath.

The beast then sneezed, almost in a derisive fashion, she thought, before lifting one of its front paws and very slowly, almost comically, taking another deliberate step forward and into the room. It was now easily within lunging distance of Grandma.

The old woman blinked slowly, almost in acknowledgment, and took a steadying breath.

Vivie realized, to her growing horror, that her life was going to change in the very next instant.

The standoff between her grandmother and the monster seemed to stretch on forever, but Vivie belatedly realized that it could not have been longer than only a few moments. The time stretched on and on, and everyone in the room seemed to be holding their breath as if waiting for some external command.

Then the wolf lunged forward, breaking the stillness. It snarled savagely as it did, going immediately for the gun. As the beast moved, Grandma fired, and the creature reeled back in shock. Blood sprayed from a wound high on its shoulder. Grandma had hit it close to the head.

Had she not taken an involuntary step back as the beast lurched towards her, she would have gotten off a clean shot and likely taken the thing down.

After the shot rang through the air, clear as a bell, the wolf grabbed the gun near the stock in its teeth and jerked its head violently from side to side. It shook the gun, and Grandma was forced to release the weapon. It clattered away on the floor, now useless.

THREE

Vivie closed her eyes tightly to avoid seeing what she knew would happen next. She began to shake violently in terror, unable to stop herself or even move from where she was rooted to the spot.

The wolf circled Grandma slowly, toying with her. Then, like lightning, it struck once, twice, and Grandma fell to the floor. She lay motionless, her eyes staring up in shock as her lifeblood drained away onto the floor, soaking the floorboards from her torn throat.

Vivie clapped her hands over her ears and moved back behind the bed and out of sight of the gruesome scene. She began to weep softly as she gently rocked herself back and forth. She clutched at her red cloak, which was tightly wound around her, desperately seeking comfort in its familiar texture.

The room was silent; not even the sound of the beast's breathing after it had killed could be heard. The damned thing didn't even appear to be winded.

It slowly circled the bed and came to stand just in front of Vivie. She suddenly realized that it was standing close to her. She could feel its hot breath on the back of her throat as it panted, and she imagined she could feel the creature opening its wide black maw filled with razor-sharp teeth to devour her. She steeled herself for the end, for what could she do if her grandmother, who knew how to use a gun and had tried to defend them, could not fend off the beast?

She squeezed her eyes shut even tighter, waiting . . . waiting. And nothing happened.

She hardly dared to breathe. Slowly, she opened her eyes. Maybe this had all been nothing but a nightmare. But as she turned towards where the creature was waiting, the hair on the back of her neck stood up, and her arms prickled with goose bumps.

She raised her eyes from the floor, and they met the eyes of the wolf. It was standing only a hair's breadth away from her face.

It was simply staring at her. Neither one of them dared to so much as blink. Vivie could feel her own eyes becoming impossibly wide in horror, and she didn't know what to do. If she moved, she felt certain the beast would attack. But she certainly couldn't stay here, pinned in terror to the floor.

She had finally steeled herself to back up slowly, cowering even further into the corner of the room when she heard footsteps outside. They were coming closer. She heard them enter the little cottage and come towards the bedroom, but she couldn't see over the bed.

The wolf snapped at her from only inches away, and she flinched back in fear, a purely instinctual reaction. But it had not gotten close enough to bite her, just close enough to scare her even more. She saw light in its blood-red eyes, almost like laughter at her fear. Then, the beast whirled, with claws and teeth flashing, towards the bedroom door and growled so deep and low that Vivie felt it rumbling inside her chest.

In one single, effortless bound, it leaped over the bed, and she felt certain that whoever had entered the house would be as doomed as she was, but there was a quick barrage of gunfire, and the beast yelped in pain and surprise. She peaked over the edge of the bed and saw a large man barring the doorway. He was dressed in green and brown hunting leathers and had a huge bushy black beard. His tiny black eyes were nearly hidden beneath a large furry hat, and his teeth were bared in a fierce, defiant grin.

"Come on, you monster! Let's see what else you've got!" He shouted.

Snarling and snapping, the wolf began a slow circle around the man. He entered the room, never taking his eyes off the beast or showing his back to it. He deftly reworked the action on his gun and reloaded it, all while focusing intently on the creature.

When he was finished reloading, he stopped walking and grinned again. "Well, come on, I haven't got all day!"

He hefted the gun to his shoulder and took careful aim at the same time that the wolf lunged across the short distance separating them. The beast was fast and managed to dodge out of the way of the first shot. But a second, well-aimed one took it low in the chest, and it tumbled to the floor. It tried to scramble to its feet but slipped on the blood, soaking the floor. It crashed down hard and snarled again, this time in frustration.

Vivie watched all of this in a sort of sick fascination. She found herself standing up and moving, almost of her feet's own accord, towards where the wolf lay on the floor. She kept staring, wide-eyed at the beast whose snarls were turning into whimpers of pain.

"Stay back, lass! He's not done yet." The man held out a hand to stop her. Yet she couldn't seem to get her feet to obey her head. Step after step, she came closer. When she was within a few feet, she stopped and could only stare as the creature in front of her died slowly.

She held out a quivering hand; it shook badly. She didn't know why she was doing it, only that she could not stop herself. *I've got to touch it to make sure this was all real.* She thought.

The man quickly moved to push her hand out of the way, but not before the wolf, in the throes of death, snapped once more and caught her hand first.

It barely broke the skin, and it didn't even hurt, Vivie thought in a disconnected way. She held up her fingers and saw small trickles of blood running down the back of her hand. She twitched her fingers experimentally and felt more blood begin to flow. She swayed on her feet and was just about to faint when strong arms enveloped her and helped ease her to the floor.

As her eyes fluttered closed, she was dimly aware of the beast as it ceased thrashing and finally lay still. It was dead, and she was safe.

And with that, she drifted off into unconsciousness.

FOUR

As Vivie slept, she had troubled dreams: dreams of running through the woods on a quiet night with the moon round and full, its light casting eerie shadows everywhere.

Some of those shadows moved. Some shadows ran from her, and larger shadows, some as big as a horse, ran behind her! The thrill of running through the forest was exhilarating. This was the adventure in life she craved!

Suddenly, she sat bolt upright in bed; she was at home, and it was morning.

Vivie looked wildly around the room in confusion. Hadn't she just been running through the forest? Being chased and chasing . . . things?

Her mother came to sit by her bedside. She used a cool cloth to mop Vivie's forehead. "It's all right now; you're safe here at home."

Vivie's eyes roved around the room, not able to focus on anything in particular. Finally, they came to rest on her father, who was sitting in his rocking chair, watching her intently. He didn't move; he smoked his pipe and stared at her.

After several long, silent moments, he stood up and walked over to her bed. He sat on the side opposite her mother and smiled kindly. "How do you feel now? We thought we were going to lose you there for a while. You didn't have any bad injuries that we could see, but you were shaken up. We thought you would die of fright."

Vivie took a deep breath and slowly exhaled. "What happened?"

Her parents looked at one another and exchanged some unspoken decisions between them.

Her father gave her mother a long, level look and then took Vivie's hands in his calloused ones, squeezing them gently. "Vivie, I'm sorry to have to tell you that your grandmother has died."

"What? How?" Vivie felt her spine go rigid as her eyes widened in shock.

Her mother asked quietly, "You don't remember anything?"

Vivie shook her head as tears began to fall onto her blanket.

Her mother rubbed her back gently to comfort her.

"It was quick," was all she said.

"She didn't . . . suffer?" Vivie could barely make herself even ask the question.

Her father glanced at her mother, but they both remained silent.

"Wha . . . what happened?" She asked them quietly, her voice barely above a whisper.

Before either one of them could answer, though, there came a loud knock on their door. Her father furrowed his eyebrows but dutifully rose to answer the door. He had to move around the other side of their kitchen, and Vivie could only make out muffled noises as he spoke to whoever was outside on the other side of the door.

Her mother continued to stroke her hair and murmured comforting words to her.

A few moments later, her father came back. He looked shaken and a little unsettled. He resumed his seat on her bed and took up her hands again.

"Who was that?" She asked him. His eyes met hers, and they were full of worry. "What's wrong, Papa?"

He shook his head and then looked at her mother. "It was Jacob Grimm, the huntsman."

"What did he want?" Her mother asked.

"Payment."

Vivie was becoming more and more confused. "Payment? For what, Papa?"

Her father heaved a sigh and tried to distract her. "Aren't you hungry? Mama will fix you some stew."

Vivie stared at the closed door and then waved a hand towards it airily. "What do you have to pay him for? Is it something I did? If it is, I'll work on my needlepoint and sell it at the market. You know the travelers enjoy hand-crafted things from our village, and I can finish a lot between now and the winter festival season."

Her father patted her hand and gave a half-hearted smile. "I appreciate it, child, but we can manage." He took a deep breath and once again looked to his wife for approval. She merely shrugged. So he nodded once and then turned back to Vivie.

"I am going to tell you what happened now because we feel you're old enough to truly understand."

Vivie tried not to look concerned and nodded slowly as he continued.

He told her the entire tale of what had happened at Grandma's house. By the time he was finished, Vivie was covering her mouth with her hand to keep from gasping in shock. Some of her dreams, it seemed, had actually been memories.

After he recounted what had happened, he continued with the aftermath.

"You remember Jacob? He often works deep in the forest, doing odd jobs, cutting wood and taking care of . . . certain unpleasant tasks. After he saved you from that monster, the huntsman carried you all the way back home."

He glanced at her mother. "And now he wants payment."

Vivie grew angry. "How much payment? He knows that no one in the village of Deyair has a lot of money."

Her mother sighed. "He wants either the money or . . . you." She broke off and stifled a little cry.

"Me? Why me?" Vivie could feel herself growing angry.

"He usually enacts payment from those he aids. It's almost always money. But sometimes, he wants something else. Or I've even heard that he's been known to trade for his work. The couple that lives down the lane paid him in eggs once, I believe. It depends on what work needs done as to what payment he requires." Her father said.

"But in this case, because you are of marrying age, he wants either his money, which is a considerable sum or your hand in marriage." Her mother finished, dabbing at her eyes with a handkerchief.

"And the fee he is requesting is . . . too high for us, my dear." Her father said softly, his eyes downcast in shame. "We cannot afford to pay him for saving you now, so we must somehow come up with a way to get him the money or else you will be forced to marry him."

Vivie was taken aback. She was only seventeen and had not even begun to think about the prospects of marriage. She knew she would eventually do so; every young girl in Deyair did, but she did not think it would happen in quite this way or this soon. *Why do I have to stay in Deyair? What if I want a different life for myself? Who says I have to marry at all?* Her thoughts raced as she became angrier.

She took a deep breath to try and steady herself. Perhaps she could reason with them.

"How long before he comes back to collect what he is owed?" Vivie heard herself ask quietly.

"By the next new moon." Her mother answered.

Vivie sighed with a small amount of relief. "That's well over a month away. I thought he would be back by the end of this week!"

Her father patted her hands and stood up. "We will try to get payment by then, so hopefully, you will not need to move out of this house just yet." He walked over to the kitchen window and looked outside. It was growing into the afternoon, and Vivie could see the rays of the sun lengthening as the sun made its journey across the sky.

"May I get out of bed?" She asked. "I want to move; my legs feel so stiff."

Her mother nodded and stood up from the bed. "Yes, but please be careful. You were unconscious when the huntsman brought you home. And you've been asleep for most of the morning. I worry that your legs won't hold you after your ordeal, and you'll fall."

Vivie huffed out a breath and stood up quickly, throwing off her blanket. "I'm fine; I don't need to be treated like a child all the time!"

Her parents both looked at her in shock; she was usually so agreeable that this sudden outburst caught them off guard.

As her mother reached for her, Vivie shrugged off her touch. "I'm fine! I feel strong and healthy."

She experimentally put weight on her left leg and then her right leg. The floor was cool beneath her toes, and so she gingerly took several steps forward as her parents watched her warily. She took some more steps, but her legs seemed solid. Her entire body felt wonderful. She must have slept well and for a long time to feel so good after such a traumatic ordeal. She twirled around in a circle, and her mother reached for her again. "I'm going outside. The sunshine looks beautiful, and I need the fresh air."

Her father shrugged, and her mother, with her mouth pressed in a thin, disapproving line, merely nodded slightly.

Vivie raced outside on legs that felt like she could jump to the moon. She dashed around their little cottage, swinging her arms, before running over to the garden and sitting on a bench there. She hugged herself and pulled her knees up to her chest as she gazed around their little farm. It wasn't much, but it was home. And after what she had witnessed, she was just thankful to be alive. *Perhaps I don't need adventure after all. I think I just want a happy life.* She thought. She looked towards the forest and suppressed a shudder. *A happy life that I choose. I can't marry that huntsman!*

She sat for a while, looking around her home and enjoying the late afternoon sunshine. Eventually, her thoughts returned to the previous day and visiting her grandmother.

At that thought, tears formed in her eyes and then fell down her cheeks. Despite surviving the attack, her grandmother did not. Her grandmother had died trying to protect her. She hugged herself and rocked back and forth as she cried.

She heard soft footsteps approaching, and she looked up to see her mother approaching, a cup in one hand and a pastry in the other. She sat down next to Vivie and offered her the pastry first.

"We never have pastries!" She smiled and started nibbling at it daintily.

Her mother returned her smile and patted her leg. "I know, but you've been through so much that I thought you deserved something extra special."

Vivie tried savoring its simple yet delicious taste but found herself gobbling it down and reaching for the cup within moments. She took a long draught of water and then wiped at her mouth with her sleeve.

Her mother chuckled. "Nerves will do that to you."

After she was finished, her mother offered her a hug, which she gratefully accepted.

FIVE

The next several days passed uneventfully. Vivie got up, as she always did, and fed the chickens. She milked their only cow and then would help her mother muck out the tiny barn they had for their animals during the winter months.

After those chores were finished, she and her mother would start in on the day's cooking by making preparations before her father would come home for lunch. When he arrived, they would all rest and eat together before resuming chores for the afternoon hours.

The days passed slowly into weeks, and all three of them focused on their immediate tasks at hand while also thinking about the upcoming payment date to the huntsman.

Vivie's father took on extra work at a neighboring farm, helping to split logs, slaughter pigs for winter, and reap hay after the harvest. When he would get home, well after dark, he was always completely exhausted.

Her mother spent time working late into the evenings every night baking and cooking things to sell at the local market. She used whatever ingredients they could spare, but even so, with their meager stores, everyone in the family was slowly growing thinner. The extra labor was causing them all to grow weaker, too.

Each Saturday morning, Vivie and her mother would go to the market, which started at dawn and went until sunset.

On one such Saturday, like all the previous Saturdays in recent weeks, Vivie and her mother walked several miles to the market in the wee hours of the morning before the sun had even crested the horizon.

It was getting cold, being early October, and Vivie hugged her red cloak tightly around herself to ward off the chill. Both she and her mother carried large baskets packed to the brim with food: cakes, pies, bread and cookies. They each also wore a rucksack filled with things like their home-made honey and a few pieces of their finest needlepoint to try and sell.

As they walked along the last bend in the road, they came upon another woman walking towards the market as well. She was bent over from a large basket she had strapped to her back with sticks in it, and she was moving slowly as if in pain. When the sound of their footsteps reached her, she turned her head away from them as they passed.

Vivie stopped, and so did her mother. "Excuse me, ma'am, but do you need help getting your wares to market?"

The woman stopped, too and reached up a hand to adjust her hood while her other hand balanced the pile of sticks on her back. Her cloak was deep blue and, despite being worn and patched in places, seemed to be of good quality. The hood hid all of her face in shadow, though.

"I appreciate your offer, but I can manage."

Vivie's mother nodded and then took her daughter's hand and began to lead her down the road again. But Vivie pulled her hand loose and gave her mother a frustrated look.

"We should help her if we are able." She muttered crossly.

"Vivie, you don't know what you're dealing with. Please, come along." Her mother hissed back.

Vivie all but stamped her foot in annoyance, petulant like a small child. "You and father always taught me to be kind."

Her mother huffed in annoyance, "Aye, but in this case, it's best to leave well enough alone."

Vivie took a few steps back towards the woman who was waiting patiently for them to finish their private discussion. She reached out a hand to assist her, but the woman brushed it away. She then reached up to readjust her hood, and Vivie caught sight of the face hidden within- her faced was horribly scarred from burns. Vivie quickly looked away in embarrassment.

The woman held up a hand, and Vivie could all but hear the smile in her voice. "It's all right, I can manage fine. Thank you, though, for your offer to help; it is appreciated."

And with that, she began to make her way down the road again, quicker this time, in order to pass Vivie's mother as she stood in the middle of the road.

Once the woman was out of earshot, Vivie rounded on her mother. "What's the matter? Why didn't you want to help her?"

Her mother shook her head aloofly and looked at the ground. "That was Kate Amana, the local witch. And no one helps her." She sniffed derisively.

Vivie thought about that for a moment and then narrowed her eyes. "But why?"

"Vivie, there are a great many things you do not know about this wide world we live in. There are a lot of dangerous things out there."

Vivie crossed her arms as her mother continued. "Remember the beast that attacked you?" Vivie nodded. "There are other things like it that lurk in that cursed forest. Vampires, werebeasts, witches, even – or so I've heard – dragons, and all manner of awful things. It's bad enough a wolf attacked you; we don't need a witch's curse on us too. For heaven's sake, leave well enough alone!"

And with that, her mother shook her head and spat on the road in the direction the woman had walked. She began walking again, although more slowly, and Vivie could tell, keeping an eye on the witch in front of them.

Confused by her mother's strong dislike of a stranger, Vivie shook her head and then hurried to catch up to her as they continued toward the market.

After a long and tiring day at the market, Vivie managed to put the encounter out of her mind. On their way home that night, Vivie and her mother discussed their sales from that day.

"I think we did quite well, Mama, don't you?"

But her mother shook her head as they trudged home. "We brought in some money, but I still don't think it's enough."

They both glanced at the sky, where the moon was rising over the horizon. It was very nearly completely black and new.

Vivie sighed.

SIX

Two days later, Vivie rose and grabbed her red cloak from its peg by the door and went out to do her morning chores. As she was finishing milking the cow, she saw a tall man walking down the road toward their cottage. She ran inside to her mother.

"Mama, mama! He's here! The huntsman is back!" She couldn't stop the icy feeling of dread forming in the pit of her stomach.

Her mother dropped the wooden spoon she was holding and whirled toward her. "Quick! Go out into the fields and fetch your father! He needs to be here for this."

At that, the girl dashed out into the field, running as fast as her legs could carry her to where her father was felling a tree at the edge of the fields.

"Papa!" She cried, almost breathless.

He turned sharply; people rarely bothered farmers while they were working as it stopped them from being as productive as they could be.

"Vivie! What a pleasant surprise!" He glanced at the sky and then frowned. "Did you bring me lunch today? It's far too early."

She came to a stop and kicked up a small cloud of dust as she did. "No, Papa, I came to tell you that the huntsman has finally come."

Her father's eyes widened in sudden shock, and he dropped the axe he had been holding. Then he shook himself to clear his thoughts and picked it up again as he moved to follow her back home. "We need to be quick about it, but I cannot keep pace with you. Go back to your mother, and I'll be along right behind you as soon as I can." He idly rubbed his left knee, still tight with pain from an old injury.

"Hurry now, he's not a man who likes to be kept waiting."

Vivie nodded, still a bit winded from her first run, and turned to race back home.

She was cresting the final hill when she saw the huntsman from afar. She squinted, trying to see if she could discern anything about this strange man, but she could not.

She saw him raise his hand to knock on the door and then turn, mid-motion, towards her. She didn't know why, but she suddenly froze in fear. She felt certain that if she moved, he would come towards her, and she really did not want that. After a moment, he seemed to lose interest in whatever he thought he saw, and so he turned back to the door to knock. Vivie was too far away to hear, but she saw the door open and assumed he exchanged a few words with her mother, who then moved to let him enter the cottage.

Vivie continued down the hill, but she now walked and felt as if she were dragging her feet. She could not place why, but she felt uneasy about meeting this man who had saved her life. *It's not that I'm afraid of marrying; I've been preparing for that most of my life.* She thought. *I can't marry him. There's something about him that's unnerving. I don't trust him.* She had no idea why she felt this way about a man she barely knew; she was familiar with his work, and he had saved her life, after all.

After what felt like hours, when she finally came to the doorway, she could hear the huntsman talking quietly with her mother. He had a soft, deep voice, but she couldn't make out exactly what he was saying. After a moment, her mother laughed, but it sounded slightly strained to Vivie's ears.

She stepped through the doorway quietly, not wanting to draw too much attention to herself. She suddenly felt shy and wanted to disappear into a corner without being noticed. But as soon as her feet crossed the threshold, his black eyes snapped to her, and she froze again.

"Why, good morning, young lady! It is a pleasure to see you again." He immediately stood up and smiled, his large furry hat in his hands.

She bobbed a short curtsey out of politeness but remained silent. He glanced at her mother, who smiled slightly. "She can sometimes be a bit shy, sir."

His grin broadened, and he took a step towards Vivie. "Don't be shy, lass, we've already met." He approached her cautiously now as if he were stalking a doe in the forest. He had left his hat on the chair where he had been sitting and now took a few slow steps towards her, an arm outstretched.

Before he was within reach of her, she instinctively flinched away from him. She could see her mother, over his broad shoulders, glaring at her in disapproval; she should be polite and gracious towards her rescuer. She looked down at the floor and rubbed one arm against the other nervously. She curled her hands into the sides of her cloak, clenching and unclenching her hands to stop them from shaking.

He stopped from a few steps away and smiled gently. "It's all right. We have plenty of time to get to know each other."

She looked up sharply at that. "Then . . . you've come for me?"

He nodded and smiled again. When he smiled, he looked only a few years older than Vivie herself. And he was quite handsome, despite the large, bushy black beard which covered most of the lower half of his face. "Aye, that I have. I saved your life, and my services cannot be without payment. I offered your parents the chance to pay me, but your mother tells me they do not have enough money."

At that, Vivie's father came to stand in the doorway. Without preamble, he entered and stood beside her, placing a firm hand on her shoulder. He glared at the huntsman. "Hello, Jacob. You are early."

The big man chuckled. "A bit, aye. But I've things to take care of deep in the woods, so I want to take her with me now. She can come along and learn some of my trade."

Vivie's eyes widened in sudden panic; she hadn't thought she would be leaving her home forever today. She looked at her father beseechingly. "Please, Papa; I'm not ready."

Her father nodded and then crossed his arms over his chest. "It is too soon, Jacob. She has not even had a chance to pack her things yet. Come back later this week, and she will go with you then." He glanced at Vivie, and she looked at the floor. She never wanted to go with this strange, wild man who made her feel wary and nervous. She somehow sensed that his calm and pleasant exterior contained a harsh and demanding interior. She was afraid of what he would turn into when they were alone together.

Jacob's eyes narrowed, and he said quietly. "No, the bargain was that you would either pay me or give her to me at the new moon. That is tonight, so your payment is due."

Her father's own eyes narrowed, and he stood firm. "I ask you to please allow us a bit more time."

The huntsman growled, low in his throat like an animal, and Vivie took a step back and away from him. "My services do not come free. And remember that I did not have to save her. Without my help, your precious daughter would now be dead. I want what I am owed as is just. Do not make me go to the local lord over such a trivial matter we can settle amongst ourselves."

Vivie's mother hurried over to stand beside her husband. "Please, sir, let us have just two more days with her? She's our only child, and we will miss her once she has gone with you."

Vivie noted, distractedly, that there didn't seem to be a question of *if* she would go with the huntsman but simply *when* she would go with him. She found that she did not like that thought at all. *Why can't I be in charge of my future? I'm not a child anymore, and I'm old enough to make my own decisions about my life.* She thought. *Why do I have to bend to the will of this strange man? True, he saved my life, but that does not give him the right to own me like a pair of boots.*

She felt her own eyes narrow as she glared at him. "Sir, if you will forgive me for saying so, but I do not feel I am quite ready to go with you." His black eyes locked onto her as she spoke. She glanced at her mother and father. "Or that I will actually go with you at all." Her mother gasped, but she kept going, "I do beg your pardon, sir, but I am not a piece of furniture to be owned. I should be able to have a say in my future."

He didn't seem to blink or move. It was as if he had suddenly been turned into a living statue. It was unsettling. She took a deep breath and stopped fiddling with her cloak. "I am truly grateful that you saved my life. It is a debt I doubt I will ever really be able to repay." She curtseyed quickly and ducked her head. "But I need time to think." After a brief hesitation, she added, "Please."

As she finished speaking, he lurched towards her, pushing both of her parents out of the way. Her mother stumbled into the table, but her father only took a few halting steps back before whirling towards the other man. The huntsman ignored him and grabbed Vivie by the arm. He squeezed ever so slightly, but it was enough to let her know that he was irritated and was not prepared to back down. She suddenly felt weak in the knees, but not from fear or the sensation that she was going to pass out; she was growing angry. And that thought startled her so much that she yelped as he squeezed again.

"Let go of her!" Her father yelled.

But the huntsman ignored him and put his face closer to hers. "You are mine." He sneered at her as she tried to pull her arm free. He then yanked her around and began to stride towards the door.

She planted her feet, but then he only dragged her. She began to twist her arm and kick at his feet, but he ignored her.

"Stop, please!" Her mother cried as she rushed the huntsman from behind. Vivie looked over her should towards the sound and saw her father try to catch her mother before she could reach them. But he was too slow, as his bad leg slowed him down. Her mother ran up behind the huntsman as he continued to drag Vivie towards the door; her red cloak flared out behind her like a banner.

When her mother reached the huntsman, she began pounding on his back with her small fists. It obviously did not hurt the big man, but he spun around and, with a free hand, backhanded her hard across the face. Vivie could hear the crack, and she screamed as her mother fell to the floor, unmoving.

She felt something inside of herself growing in rage. She struggled even harder and managed to rake her nails across the huntsman's big hands as she continued to kick at him. As he pulled her in close to his body to keep her still, she whipped around and bit him on the back of one burly hand. He bellowed like a bull and suddenly dropped her. As he cradled his hand, he snarled at her in incoherent fury. As their eyes met, he suddenly froze in shock. His tiny black eyes widened, and he quickly backed away from her in alarm.

She stood there, breathing raggedly and bared her teeth at him. She was dimly aware of her father pulling her mother out of further harm's way.

The huntsman took a deep breath and straightened, standing to his full, tall height. He was no longer cradling his injured arm, and it dangled, forgotten, at his side. Instead, he was now staring at her with wariness. "Your eyes . . ." He whispered.

She grunted but did not otherwise move or acknowledge him.

His eyes narrowed, and his uninjured hand went towards a large hunting knife he had strapped to his leg. Her eyes tracked his every motion. He glanced over his shoulder towards her father. "Do not move, do not even breathe. If you let me claim her as my bride and take her with me today, I will heal her right now."

Her father looked up from where he crouched on the floor, tears streaming down his face as if he hadn't heard the huntsman speak. "She's dead. You killed her." He rocked Vivie's mother's still form back and forth in his arms.

The huntsman made a shushing sound and turned back to keep an eye on Vivie.

"Leave her; we've got bigger problems to deal with now. Your daughter is . . ." But he didn't get the chance to finish because, with a roar, Vivie's father launched himself at the huntsman's unprotected back. He leaped up onto the huntsman's back and began beating the man with his fists in his neck, arms, anywhere he could reach.

The huntsman spun around and pushed Vivie's father off of him. He was brandishing the naked blade that Vivie hadn't seen him draw because it was so fast. "Papa, no!" She screamed.

Her father rushed at the huntsman again without pause or care, and the huntsman reacted purely on instinct, his muscle memory ingrained from his trade. He brought the weapon up to protect himself. His large body blocked whatever happened next, but Vivie heard her father scream in pain and shock. She heard a grunt and then a heavy thud.

She could see her father's body now, lying sprawled on the floor at the huntsman's feet.

The huntsman quickly turned around to face her again as his knife dripped blood onto the floor. As she stared at her father's body in shock, her eyes snapped to the still form of her mother.

Dead. Both of her parents were dead. Killed right in front of her by this hulking beast of an inhumane man. Too quickly and too brutally for her to fully comprehend. In the blink of an eye, in the span of a heartbeat, she was now alone.

Who is this wild man anyway? Who does he think he is to have all this power? She wondered. He was a stranger who roamed the forests looking for cheap work, doing jobs no one else wanted to do, and then preying on the weak and helpless when he did decide to offer his aid to those poor people who had no choice but to sell their meager rations of food or wares for their safety.

Vivie saw red for the first time in her life. Her hands clenched and unclenched spastically at her sides, then she felt herself curving her fingers into claws as her rage grew.

She could hear, distantly, the sound of ripping cloth and knew she was inadvertently shredding her red cloak in her growing fury. She didn't care. She realized she didn't care about anything anymore: not her grandmother, nor her parents, not even herself and her safety or future. There was no more meaning in her pitiful life, and she didn't care.

Her eyes narrowed to slits and stayed locked on the man before her. There was a low, huffing, grating sound, and she realized belatedly that she was growling. Then, her eyesight went completely dark red, and she was unaware of what happened next.

SEVEN

The huntsman watched in silent revulsion and slowly began to back away from her. He stared at her as a spasm of pain hit her, and she clutched at her stomach before rearing back in sudden surprise. Her red cloak flared out behind her, waving like a bright red standard behind her. Then she dropped to all fours and crouched on the floor, her hands scratching at the dirt floor, red cloak pooled around her like blood.

She began to shiver violently all over as if her entire body were tingling with unseen energy. He watched in horror as her skin began to ripple and move of its own accord. Her eyes snapped open then, and she stared around the room in wide-eyed confusion. He could see that her eyes were no longer the lovely shade of hazel that they had been when they'd first met but were now a sullen, glowing, evil red color. Her back arched, and her simple, homespun dress split down the back with a horrible ripping sound.

He could see tiny, dark hairs begin to sprout all over her arms and legs that poked out from the cloak as she thrashed around. He had now backed away from her as far as he could go and had placed the table and the two bodies between them. He glanced towards the door: too far to run. Besides, if he ran away into the growing evening, she would chase him down. No, he had to finish this here and now.

When his eyes returned to her, she was curled up on the floor, nothing but a lump under the red cloak. She was making pained, mewling noises in the back of her throat. They didn't sound like anything a human throat could make. He couldn't actually see any of her skin from this angle anymore, but he heard the sickening sounds of bones breaking, popping and reforming, and he knew he only had moments.

He began to creep towards the door. He kept up a slow and steady shuffle, trying to be as quiet as possible and not draw any more unwanted attention to himself as he kept inching closer and closer toward the door. If he could get outside, he would have much more room to maneuver than in this tiny cottage.

Halfway to the door, he froze and stared at the suddenly still and silent form. A long nose poked itself free of the remains of the cloak as scraps of red fabric fell to the floor. It made wet snuffling sounds as it twitched and inhaled. A deep and menacing growling sound followed. Suddenly, the creature burst forth from the tattered shreds, bits of fabric raining down like droplets of crimson rain. It was free at last.

What stood before him could only be described as something out of a nightmare. And not just a child's nightmare either, but something primal and deadly, something that lurks in the darkness of even the most steadfast of adults' dreams.

It was a wolf, although much larger than any normal wolf he'd ever seen. He placed it at well over one hundred pounds. And it was covered in thick, shaggy, black fur. Almost comically, a shred of the destroyed red cloak still clung around its neck, like a bright splash of strawberry juice against the dark fur.

Its long tail lashed angrily from side to side, and its pointed ears flicked idly at sounds as it inhaled again deeply. Its paws were huge, tipped with long black claws meant for slashing prey. Its muzzle was filled; he knew from past experiences with normal wolves with razor-sharp teeth meant to rend and devour. He could see the top fangs poking down over its lower lip from where he stood, and he shuddered involuntarily.

He stood, frozen in both wonder and fear, rooted to the spot. He had seen many things in his days as a hunter and forester, but the beasts of the local woods always fascinated him the most. This was a creature meant only to destroy and kill anything that crossed its path. He had to respect its simple, raw and deadly power.

He also realized that he had to get out of there as soon as possible. The huntsman took another halting step towards the door. An ear twitched in his direction, and he froze again, mid-motion. The beast's eyes snapped towards him and locked onto him. It growled again, low and full of hatred.

He huffed out a breath he hadn't known he'd been holding. "Alright, girly, let's you and me dance."

The wolf woofed in agreement and charged him, jaws snapping. He whirled towards the open door and sprinted outside. As he exited the cottage, he continued across the little front yard and then spun around to face the beast nipping at his heels.

The wolf skidded to a halt a few yards away, stopping to stare at him. The way this creature was acting was alarming as he had never experienced something quite like this before. Wild wolves and beasts of the forest he knew how to deal with. He'd even dealt with a few supernatural things. But this creature was different. It seemed almost unsure as to how a wild wolf should act. Trying to make decisions as if it had a mind behind those bloodred eyes.

He leaned forward and bent his knees, balancing on the balls of his feet, a pose meant to allow him to move quickly into changing directions. Being faster than the wolf might help keep him alive. He held his still bloodied knife in one hand and drew a billy club that he carried with his other hand. He would have preferred another knife or, better yet, one of his many guns. But he had come as close to unarmed as he ever traveled to this cottage, and he was, not for the first time today, seriously regretting it.

The wolf continued to stare at him, and he felt himself begin to sweat. The beast inhaled again and then made a coughing sound that, he thought, somehow conveyed a sound of amusement. He knew it could smell his unease, and it was pleased that he was afraid.

His eyes narrowed in annoyance. Why should he, a mighty huntsman, be troubled by a mere beast of the forest? He was known throughout the land as a skilled hunter, a fearless man who spent much of his time in the dark, dangerous woods all alone. But he also knew that he had to be careful. One bite or scratch from this monster in this form and he would become just like it. And that was never going to happen.

"Come on, I haven't got all day!"

The wolf charged then, coming towards him low and fast. It was an amateur move, and so he easily sidestepped and danced away, out of range of the snapping jaws. He wanted to tire it out into making a mistake. Being rash or over-eager for the kill, while being its own kind of pleasure for him, would be a huge mistake on his part and, likely, his very last.

He motioned with his billy club, trying to taunt the beast. "Too slow there on your new paws, eh?"

The wolf whirled and charged again, barely pausing to turn around. It moved incredibly fast, even being new to running on four legs. He was surprised by this; other newly changed beasts that he had encountered tended to be ungainly, confused and slow. This one seemed born to this form already. It was creepy, and he knew that with this one, he'd need to be exceptionally cautious.

He taunted the animal again, trying to buy himself some more time, "I came here for you today, girly or payment for my work. If I cannot have either one, killing a monster like you will suffice instead. And I won't sleep any less easy for the pleasure of ending your life." The wolf snarled, and he continued, enjoying baiting the beast. "Your grandmother was a fool, an unprofessional who didn't know what she was doing, and it got her killed. She should have known her place. She should have left this sort of work to a man: a professional who is stronger, smarter and faster than a mere *woman*."

That must have struck a nerve because the wolf rushed him again, this time with its mouth gaping towards him, going towards his midsection. It was a more powerful attack, meant to drive him back so the creature could go for his throat instead of simply trying to catch him off balance. It was not an amateur move.

His eyes narrowed in concentration, and he held the beast off of him using his knife and billy club crossed in front of himself. He was a big man, it was true and had a lot of muscle from working endless hours of hard labor, but this wolf was easily the size of a pony and was packed with natural muscle in its own right. And it was angry, so angry that saliva dribbled from its jaws as it snapped at his hands. He managed to force it away again, though and took several steps backwards. Now, the cottage was behind him.

He chanced a glance over one shoulder. If he could get to the door before the beast could, he could throw the bolt home and be safe for the night. He knew the wolf would eventually grow bored and leave. But he turned towards the wolf again and grunted. Running would not allow him the satisfaction of killing this monster. He did so enjoy dispatching these sorts of creatures. It gave him a fierce sort of pleasure at ending another's life that he suddenly grinned. Nor would running and hiding gain him any more notoriety and fame. If he had those, people would seek him out for more jobs. And more jobs meant a better income. No, he needed to end this thing now.

So, he taunted it yet again, which, he knew somewhere in his mind, was often a very bad idea. But he didn't care; killing was an indulgence he didn't get to enjoy as often as he would have liked. "And your mum and pop were fools too. They couldn't just give me what I was owed." He gave a half-hearted shrug.

The wolf growled again, and its tail stood out straight behind it, stiff as a bottle brush, which was a sure sign the beast was growing more and more livid. Its red eyes glowed dangerously.

It paused for a heartbeat and then lunged forward again. This time, it was also aiming for his midsection, which he found odd; the same two tricks, one right after the other? But just before its sharp teeth could connect with his arm, the wolf's head dipped low, and it went for his ankles to try to sweep his feet out from under him.

He brought his knife up hard into its shoulder. They connected hard, and he was knocked to the ground. They rolled together, and he brought his knife up to protect himself again.

The blade bit deep into the wolf's shoulder again, and the beast bellowed in pain. It sprang away and circled him again. Now, it limped on an injured left front leg from a gaping wound on its shoulder. The blood ran down to its paw and puddled on the dry ground.

The creature's eyes narrowed, and he could barely even see a hint of red. For a moment, he thought it had closed its eyes in silent surrender. But then, it lunged forward again.

This time, it went straight toward his knife hand. There was no evasion and no preamble at a feint, and it was an obvious move. So, before it could take off his hand at the wrist, the huntsman brought his billy club up and smashed it into the side of the wolf's head. Stunned, the beast fell to the huntsman's side as he tumbled to the ground.

Instead of staggering to its feet, the wolf lay on its side, whimpering.

He knew better than to approach it, though, so he stood up slowly and dusted the earth from his pants. He kept an eye on the beast at all times as he did so, but it didn't move any further.

He huffed indignantly. "The least you could do is put up a decent fight, you stupid girl."

He waited, but nothing happened; no reaction.

He shrugged to himself and slowly walked towards the creature, extending both of his weapons in case it decided to rush him again.

As the huntsman stood over the beast, he didn't detect any twitch of movement. It lay still and unmoving. It barely seemed to breathe. Perhaps he had clubbed it harder than he had intended. He glared at it in anger. "I had thought to have a good go with you. But I guess you're as worthless as your kin. Bah, have done with ye!"

He was angry now. Angry at having been denied his payment, angry at losing a bride he was hungry for, angry at being out at this hour and away from his proper duties; he was just an angry man. He snarled, and spit flew from his lips as he spent his rage.

The wolf stared at him through red eyes, unmoving and accepting of her fate. So rather than simply ending her life and suffering, the huntsman, in his cruelty, did not run her through with his knife, as he normally might have with such a nightmarish creature.

Instead, he raised the billy club slowly in front of her eyes so that she could see it. Then, he brought it down again and again and again all over her body. He kicked at her with his boots, breaking ribs. He smashed her skull, swelling an eye shut and tearing an ear. He beat her, and yet the wolf never made a single sound. He would remember it later as being incredibly eerie.

When he had worn out his frustration, he kicked the body once more for good measure and then stomped off towards his own home. Let the forest creatures have whatever was left of the beast; he was satisfied that his job was finished.

EIGHT

Something was hard beneath her head, and she didn't like it; it was uncomfortable. She could hear birdsong somewhere nearby, and it made her head pound with a headache. She huffed in indignation at being woken up from a sound sleep. Her sides ached, too. She tried to move her left leg because she couldn't feel it, but it wouldn't respond to her thoughts. She kept her eyes shut tight and inhaled as deeply as she could: pine. It smelled like the deep forest, warm sunshine (which she could also feel on the side of her body) and dry earth beneath her. That, at least, was a small comfort. Other than the pain she was now feeling all over, things seemed normal.

She slowly opened her eyes. Or rather, tried to open both of them. Her right eye was swollen completely shut, and she bared her teeth in discomfort over that realization. Her other eye looked at the open sky and saw a flock of birds flying far overhead. She blew out a breath, which hurt, and raised her head slowly. As soon as she moved, her limited vision swam, so she put her head back down on the ground and closed her unswollen eye.

She woke again to the sound of birdsong, only this time, it was the cawing of ravens and crows. She inhaled gingerly and smelled the oncoming twilight: dusk smelled cool and inviting.

Her stomach rumbled, and she opened her eye again, remembering that her other eye was hurt. It was becoming evening; the sun was setting, and the birds who had woken her with their noise were circling too close for comfort.

She again picked her head up, and it still hurt. It felt like her brain was stuffed full of cotton, and she couldn't seem to remember anything other than waking up in the forest just now.

She inhaled again, only this time a bit more deeply. That also hurt, and she grunted in annoyance. She looked up to see the flock of ravens and crows circling lower and lower over where she lay. That was odd; those birds normally only did that over dead or dying things. She shook her head slightly, and her ears rang.

She looked around; she was out in the middle of a clearing with the forest's trees off to her right. Far enough away, she would need to do a quick jog to get back into the safety of the trees. On her other side was a small structure. As her nose took in information about her surroundings, she looked toward the structure and could smell only death there. She sneezed in disgust involuntarily, and the motion sent waves of pain radiating throughout her body. Whatever the structure was, there was nothing there for her.

But she couldn't continue to lay here out in the open, exposed. Who knew how long she had been out here and helpless already? She was lucky nothing had come along to finish her off yet. So, she tested first her back legs and then her front legs. Her left front leg was numb from her shoulder down. That wasn't good, so she had to be extra careful until it had time to heal itself.

She checked behind herself, too; her tail hung limp and sad behind her. She twitched it experimentally; it still worked, although it hurt at the base to move it.

Satisfied that she wouldn't immediately be a meal for the crows and ravens, she began to make her way toward the safety of the trees slowly. It seemed to take forever, with her never actually getting any closer. But as she limped along, she knew that she had to be getting closer as the shadows of the trees were lengthening. And, once she was safe again in the forest, she could lay down to rest. She hadn't realized how exhausted she felt.

Once she finally crossed the threshold of the trees, she found a large pine tree and pushed the lowest hanging branches away with her nose. She delicately eased herself to the ground and promptly fell into a deep sleep.

She was dimly aware of someone singing. It was not birdsong this time, but words. Something about the sun and the rain and the apple seeds. She shook her head and opened her eyes. It was morning, and the sun was shining, trying to filter through the woods. She could see it between the branches that shaded her now.

A young man was walking along the path out in the field before her. He was thin and ragged looking, with a cloth bag slung over one shoulder. And he was wearing something metal on his head. Despite his clothes being in disrepair, the thing on his head shone like polished moonlight.

He was singing and waving his hands about behind him, occasionally reaching into his bag. His singing was not particularly good, she thought, but at least he sounded happy. Perhaps he could tell her why she hurt so badly.

She crept out of her hiding place and found that she could move a little easier. She still hurt and was badly stiff, but at least she wasn't about to pass out from the pain now. She woofed with a small amount of satisfaction.

At the sound, the young man whirled around to face her. His eyes widened, and one of his hands went to the silver thing on his head. He took it off and began twirling it around in his hands nervously.

She sat down and tilted her head to one side. She asked him, "Please, sir, could you tell me why I am so badly hurt? I don't remember anything at all, and it's beginning to scare me. I think I need help."

His eyes widened even more, and now he held the silver thing in his hands like a weapon, brandishing it at her and making shooing noises. She tilted her head to the other side.

"G . . . g . . . go away w . . . w . . . wolfy. I've no m . . . m . . . meat for you." He stammered. She inhaled sharply; he smelled ripe with fear, and her stomach rumbled.

He took a sharp breath, and his knobby knees began knocking together audibly.

"Sir, I beg of you, please help me." She said as slowly and clearly as she could.

He shook his head vigorously from side to side in confusion. Apparently, he could not understand what she was saying, although she could understand him perfectly. That was strange.

She looked down at herself and raised her left front paw to show him she was hurting. Then, she whimpered softly.

The whimpering must have done it because his mouth opened to form a little 'o' shape, and she realized he was surprised. For some reason, he was afraid of her, and she couldn't figure out why.

Reluctantly, he knelt on the ground and beckoned her to come forward. She did, slowly and with her head and tail hanging low. She had to limp as well, which could only have aided in her pathetic appearance.

Once she reached him, he ran a hand over her body, and she flinched whenever he touched a place that hurt, which, unfortunately, was most of her body. She let slip a soft growl, and when she did, he snatched his hand back quickly, his eyes widening in panic. But she thumped her tail once, and he calmed down again to resume his examination.

He gently prodded her injured shoulder and tsked as the open wound seeped some fresh blood. She winced but, this time, did not growl at him. He seemed genuinely interested in helping her.

"I cannot patch you up, but I can give you something small to eat." He reached into his bag and drew out a red, round blob. It smelled crisp and green, similar to the forest itself. She took it gently from his open palm and then began to gnaw on it, taking little strips off the outside and then licking the juicier inside.

"That is called an apple." He said slowly and enunciating the word. She huffed indignantly. Of course, she knew what an apple was. They grew on several trees deep within the forest. There were usually deer nearby, too, who liked to snack on them in the autumn.

"Oh yes, of course, you'd know what an apple is." He scratched the back of his head idly as he fished another one out of his bag. "But apples are all I have, I'm afraid."

She wagged her tail to show her appreciation, and he smiled.

Then he looked around as if they were being watched by something. "I can't stay here long; I've got to sow the apple seeds. And while I cannot help you with your injuries, I can tell you that deep in the forest lives . . ." He paused and glanced around again as if someone would overhear them. "A witch. It is said that she can heal animals. And since she lives all alone, she often enjoys their company." He pointed north into the trees. "Go due north until you come to the old oak tree that's split and burnt from a lightning strike; you should be able to smell the smoke from her cottage from there. Just follow your nose."

She wagged her tail again and stood up. She only staggered a little this time, and she nodded at him before turning and heading north into the forest.

NINE

It was getting on towards midday when she stopped at a stream to slake her thirst. The sun had risen, high and bright in the sky, and she felt content in the darker recesses of the woods.

The sunlight dappled the leaves of the trees and shone like gold in the reflections of the water. She leaned over to take a drink and stopped short; she was a frightful sight. Her good eye stared back at her, bright and curious, but her right eye was still horribly swollen, and she couldn't see out of it. She noticed that her left ear was torn and had dried blood crusted on it, too. It also looked like parts of her face, including her muzzle, were swollen or beginning to swell. Her fur was also matted in many places from dried blood and time spent lying in the dirt. And those were just the injuries she could see on her face.

She made a disgusted sound and then began drinking the water. She lapped up the crystal-clear water, taking a moment to sit and enjoy the quiet stillness of the forest around her as her beaten body ached in protest at every movement she made.

When she was finished, she lay down again in the shade and began meticulously grooming her matted black fur. She started with where she could easily reach without causing herself too much pain: her face and front paws. Then she moved on to her back legs and tail. It was hard to twist around and reach her tail with her ribs burning in discomfort, but she managed.

Once she was finished, she felt remarkably better, and she sighed in contentment. Even if it wasn't as impeccable as she would have preferred, at least it was something.

Her stomach made a gurgling sound, and a nearby bird, which was sitting in a tree, fluttered into startled flight. She huffed out a laugh and rose, thinking to seek out some food. The apples, while sweet and a new flavor for her, had not sustained her for long.

She still had a bad limp, and she had to rest frequently, which made her progress incredibly slow, but she began to make her way deeper into the forest. After what seemed like days of slogging through the growing dimness, she finally realized she could go no further, so she flopped down among the ferns and instantly fell asleep.

There was sunlight shining down on her, and she squeezed her eyes shut tighter against it. And something was dripping nearby: an irksome, repetitive, plinking sound. She growled softly in annoyance, and she heard a sudden, sharp intake of breath very close to her.

Her single, un-swollen eye snapped open. She was still deep in the woods, and she was laying on her right side among the underbrush. But she was not alone anymore.

A woman, who was wearing a deep blue cloak and whose cowl cast her entire face deeply in shadow, was sitting calmly beside her. She could make out the woman's chin and mouth.

And she was easily within biting distance. After a moment of stillness from them both, as they stared at each other, frozen, the woman resumed whatever it was she was doing.

She felt gentle, warm hands probing her body, and she stiffened reflexively. The woman continued what she was doing, either ignoring or unaware of her actions. Then, the woman began to hum softly. The sound was low and pleasant at first and then grew in intensity until she felt herself making an almost purring sound with pleasure at the sound. The music filled the little clearing she was lying in, and it began to fill her with a warm sensation, which was very welcome indeed.

When she looked at whatever the woman was doing, craning her head around, she saw little motes of light flitting around near the woman's long-fingered hands. They glowed like tiny lightning bugs and cast showers of sparks in the air. She watched, fascinated.

The light went to the various parts of her body that hurt or ached, and she immediately felt flashes of sharp, intense heat. There were bright flashes of radiance at each point one of the little lights touched, and then the pain, in its various places, eased a little. The woman was healing her.

She felt her tail thump appreciatively, and then she could hear a note of pleasure creep into the woman's song. The woman was pleased that the wolf was remaining still and almost sounded relieved at her acceptance and gratitude.

After what seemed like only a moment, the woman suddenly slumped to the side, taking her wonderfully warm hands away. The wolf looked up; the woman was exhausted and did not move. She could see that the woman was still breathing, though, so she moved around to get more comfortable and then laid her head in the woman's lap. It was a sign of thanks. The woman brought one of her hands up languorously and stroked the fur near the wolf's ears. The wolf wagged her tail in pleasure and fell into a deep, restful sleep.

When she awoke, it was growing dark again. The woman was still sitting beside her, apparently also asleep. Her breathing was slow and calm, and the wolf could see her chest rising and falling smoothly.

She slowly removed her head from the woman's lap and then stood up, testing each leg and paw systematically. She was sore, certainly, but the glaring pains had faded to aches. Her shoulder and front leg still hurt a lot, but she knew she would be able to walk faster than before, even if she would still have a limp. Perhaps she would have that for the rest of her life.

She inhaled deeply and sighed with pleasure. She felt so much better. And it was all thanks to this strange woman.

She nosed gently at the woman, and she moved in her sleep. The woman's hood, which had been hiding most of her face, fell to the side, and the wolf was finally able to see who had saved her life.

She had beautiful, long red hair, and she had smile lines around her eyes. She might once have been breathtakingly beautiful if it weren't for the horrible scars down one side of her lovely face. They were burn scars.

Suddenly, her eyes snapped open, and she made a little 'oh' sound of surprise at having her patient so close to her face. She reached up to replace her hood, but the wolf nosed her hand away. They stayed like that, staring at each other. The woman's dark brown eyes furrowed in confusion, and she tilted her head to the side and asked, "Can you understand me?"

The wolf very slowly nodded her head up and down. The woman smiled broadly. "I knew you weren't just an ordinary wolf! Here, come with me. I have herbs back at my cottage and a potion that will help us." She rose to her feet and began walking off into the woods, heading north.

TEN

The wolf followed the woman, really, because she had nothing else to do. And this was obviously the witch the young man had told her about. Even if it wasn't, what did she have to lose since this woman had healed her?

She padded silently behind the woman, dutifully following her blue cloak through the twists and turns of a well-worn path through the trees. After a few moments, they came upon a tiny cottage nestled deep within the trees. It had a thatched roof and a column of smoke lazily curled skyward from the little chimney. The walls were impeccably white-washed and clean, and she could smell dried herbs coming from inside.

The woman walked inside, and when she reached the doorway, she turned around to see if the wolf had followed her. "Please, do come in. I am Kateryn Amana, but most people call me Kate."

The wolf followed her into a delightfully quaint little home. The cottage only had one small room. A pallet was against the right wall as she entered, made all neat with a heavy blanket on top. In the back left corner was the kitchen. Next to that was a small countertop and table by a large fireplace set into the back wall. The dried herb smell was coming from the rafters, where dozens of types of plants of every description were hanging upside-down, drying and at various stages of completion. There were so many different types that the wolf could not begin to identify even half of them, although her nose told her they were all special.

Her eyes came to rest expectantly on the woman, who was taking off her cloak. She hung it up on a peg by the door and then brushed her hands down her simple light blue dress and white apron.

"I was out gathering more herbs, you see." She pulled out still more herbs that had been hidden in the pockets of her cloak. She went to the kitchen counter and used a pitcher to pour water over them. She rubbed her hands over them, cleaning them. When she was satisfied, she used some twine to tie them together and then hung those, too, from the rafters.

The wolf sat down just inside the doorway and watched all of this with her head tilted in interest.

"I do have to wonder where you came from though. You're not just another wolf since I've tended one or two of those in my time as well. I wonder where you came from."

She talked over her shoulder as she began going back and forth to shelves over the kitchen counter. She opened bottles and tankards and jars full of . . . the wolf had no idea what, though some of them smelled rank, and she wrinkled her nose in disgust.

The woman pulled this and that out of containers and moved everything onto the table. She even brought over a kettle that had been hovering over the fire on a long metal pole. The wolf seemed mildly alarmed at this, and her ears went back slightly. Kate held up a hand, "Don't worry; the hot water is just for my tea." She smiled and continued to work.

At some point, the wolf got tired of watching whatever it was the woman was doing, so she went over to the fireplace and lay down. The warmth of the fire quickly lulled her into sleep.

Her nose twitched . . . something smelled savory. Then, her stomach growled. She was starving. She opened an eye and found herself still on the floor by the fireplace at the healer's cottage. She raised her head to find Kate sitting in a chair on the other side of her, opposite the corner of the little cottage's kitchen. She was sitting in a rocking chair and was rocking gently back and forth. She had a book in her hands, and her brow was furrowed intently as she muttered occasionally to herself.

She paused in her reading and glanced up when she felt the wolf watching her. "Awake again? Ah, good. I know you need your sleep to help you heal, but you can't simply sleep forever. Or else you may end up like that Aurora girl and sleep all of the time!" She shook her head in disapproval. "Besides, we've work to do, and it's much more exciting than sleeping."

She stood up and walked over to the wolf, kneeling to look her in the eye. "I know you're hurting, but I need you to trust me for just a little while longer, all right?"

The wolf nodded, slowly bobbing her shaggy head up and down once.

Kate then moved to the table and poured something into a large bowl. The wolf came to stand beside her and cocked her head in confusion. "It's all right; it's supposed to bubble like that."

The wolf sighed, clearly not believing her. "No, really. It's only gone wrong if that smoke turns purple." The smoke did not turn purple. Instead, it popped and fizzed and then turned blue as it billowed over the edges of the table and onto the floor. The wolf took a few steps back in alarm.

Kate chuckled. "It's all right, I promise." She smirked. "Besides, if I had wanted to hurt you, why on earth would I have helped heal you yesterday?"

The wolf made a woofing sound, acknowledging the truth of that statement, and then sat down. Though she was still not that close to the table as she continued to watch.

After another few moments, Kate brought her hands up and held them over the bowl. She began chanting rhythmically. The wolf whimpered, but she ignored her.

Finally, with one last murmured word that somehow echoed off the walls, the potion puffed a bright white, and the light faded, and then there was silence.

Kate took the bowl in both hands and carefully placed it on the ground near the wolf's paws. After a moment, she said, "Well, go ahead."

The wolf tilted her head this way and that and eyed the bowl skeptically.

Kate sat down on the floor on the other side of the bowl, and her skirts billowed out around her. She nudged the bowl with her foot. "Go on, then." Kate folded her hands in her lap and smiled. "Come on, it's not going to hurt you. As I've already said, if I had wanted to actually hurt you, there's no reason why I would have helped you first." She sighed. "This potion will allow me to understand you. It's from a modified telepathy spell my grandmother taught me when I was eight."

The wolf stared at her but then slowly nodded once. She lapped up the liquid and, after a few sips, sneezed uproariously several times. She shook herself vigorously and then sat back down, once again staring at Kate. "Achoooo!" Kate heard in her mind.

"My goodness, bless you!" She chuckled.

"The bubbles tickled," came the reply.

She laughed and offered the wolf her hand to sniff. "How about a proper introduction, eh?"

When the wolf didn't move, she put her hand back in her lap. "You're definitely not a wolf, are you?"

"I . . . I don't know," was the answer.

Now, it was Kate's turn to tilt her head. "What do you mean, you don't know? How can you not know whether or not you started this life as what you currently are?"

The wolf huffed in frustration, and Kate smiled sympathetically.

"Do you have anything that can help me to remember?" The wolf asked.

Kate shook her head. "No, I'm sorry. Messing with memories is a tricky business. And sometimes we should forget." She reached up and absentmindedly traced some of the scars on the left side of her face.

The wolf nudged her hand away with her nose and then licked her face. "Oh, it doesn't hurt anymore. It happened so long ago." There was still pain in her eyes. "But I still remember it often." She blinked her eyes quickly a few times and sighed. "Best not to dwell on such things; it's in the past now."

Kate moved to stand up, but the wolf grabbed one of her hands in her teeth. The gesture was gentle and did not break the skin; it was meant to reassure. "I am sorry." The wolf said in her mind.

Kate nodded and patted the wolf on the head with her other hand. "It's all right. Now, let's get some lunch. I'm sure you're still very hungry." This time, she did stand up, and she moved to the kitchen counter again. She brought out a few vegetables, which she cut and placed in a bowl for herself. Then she went to the ice box in the corner and came back with a small parcel wrapped in wax paper. When she opened it, the wolf began to drool. Inside were the remains of a chicken.

Kate placed the meat in another bowl and then put that on the floor. She had scarcely gotten her hands out of the way when the wolf came over and gobbled the food down in large gulps.

She took her own meager helping to the small table, sat down and then tucked into her meal.

When they were both finished (and the wolf had licked her bowl clean and come over to lick Kate's, too), they sat down by the fire together. Kate rocked in her chair, her hand idly stretched out to scratch the wolf behind her ears. Her tail wagged in pleasure, and she sighed contentedly.

The pair of them sat like that into the growing evening, comfortable with the crackle of the fire and the rhythmic squeaking of the rocking chair. Finally, Kate stopped rocking and peered over the side of the chair to look at the wolf.

"What exactly shall I call you?" She tapped a finger to her lips in thought. "I cannot very well simply call you 'she' and 'wolf' if we're to get to know each other better." She gave the wolf a long and level look. "And I assume you're going to be staying with me for a while."

The wolf glanced out the door and then back to match her gaze. "I honestly have nowhere else I would know to go to," came the voice in Kate's mind.

Kate reached out and petted her head. "It's all right; we can keep each other company." She looked around the small cottage and smiled halfheartedly. "Honestly, sometimes I wish I had more company. I get so lonely from time to time. And while helping the animals of the forest does bring me into contact with others, it never lasts long since they're wild animals." She glanced back at the wolf. "But you're certainly not wild." She chuckled. "A wild wolf would never have let me poke and prod them for as long as you did. So either you're tamed or were so badly injured as not to have any idea what I was doing."

The wolf slowly shook her head. "I . . . remember something." Kate nodded and made a motion with one hand for her to continue. "But . . . it's fuzzy." The wolf sneezed.

"You were hurt badly, including your head, which seems to have affected your memories," Kate said. "Perhaps it will come back in time."

The wolf nodded slowly, then tilted her head. "What do you wish to call me?"

Kate thought for a moment, and then a slow smile spread across her lips. "I know just the name! Since I do not know what you may have been called in your other life, I shall call you 'Whisper.'"

The wolf tilted her head. "Why?"

Kate laughed. "Because you're certainly quieter than any wolf has any right to be. You were calm as a whisper while I was healing you, never making a sound. And your eyes are full of secret whispers." She smirked and laid a gentle finger on the wolf's nose. The wolf's eyes crossed as she followed Kate's finger. She shook her head and sat back. Then, she wagged her tail.

"All right, I shall be Whisper."

ELEVEN

They spent the next several days falling into what would become a common routine. In the morning, just before dawn, they would both rise and go out to take care of the few chickens Kate had. She even had a small chicken coop and yard behind her cottage.

Kate would feed them and collect a few eggs while Whisper would watch the forest for any signs of danger. (Danger never actually found them this way, but the wolf was too tempted by the chickens and so had to focus her attention elsewhere while Kate did the actual work.)

She also seemed to crave to be near Kate at all times and had taken it upon herself to be the healer's companion and bodyguard.

One day, while they were both inside the cottage, her ears perked up as she heard someone crying off in the distance. It was coming from down the worn path and off into the dense undergrowth in the forest.

Whisper glanced at Kate, but she was indulging in more reading, so the wolf tugged her sleeve and then went outside by herself.

She followed the sound until she came to a small clearing where a little boy wearing red pants and a black jacket was sitting with his back to her. He was also wearing a pointed hat, which the wolf tilted her head; some people who had an odd sense of fashion.

He was sitting on a fallen log and was sobbing into his hands. He had no idea she was there. She crept forward slowly, trying not to make a sound, though she needn't have bothered; the boy was absorbed in his sadness and paid no attention to what was around him.

She came to stand in front of him and sat down across from him, leaving a respectful amount of space between them. She thought that some semblance of distance might make him feel better when he realized that he was alone in the forest with a large predator sitting before him.

She watched and waited; finally, she woofed softly. It was low and patient-sounding, but the little boy was startled anyway.

She thumped her tail, and it rustled fallen leaves where she was sitting. She stayed absolutely still and waited.

The little boy froze, his dark brown eyes wide and frightened. But after a few long, strained moments, he seemed to relax a little and looked around the clearing. It was almost as if he expected someone else to appear and tell him it was all a grand joke.

Whisper waited patiently until the little boy's gaze returned to hers. When he didn't look like he was going to pass out from fear or bolt in terror from her (which is generally unwise to do around predators), she stood up and moved towards him. She kept her movements extremely slow and deliberate so as not to spook him into flight.

When she was within touching distance of him, she sat down again and wagged her tail. Other than that, she continued to wait.

He tentatively reached out a shaking hand and touched the ruff of fur around her neck. The black fur was deep and soft, and he made a sound of delight in the back of his throat. He gently fingered the red ribbon around her neck but didn't tug on it.

His tears had left dirt tracks down his cheeks, and he snuffled every so often, but at least he had stopped crying.

After a few moments of sitting peacefully, Whisper rose and, very gently, took the edge of his black jacket between her teeth. He stiffened as soon as she moved, but once he saw that she did not intend to hurt him, he also stood up. She tugged at his clothing and then walked a few paces away and looked back at him over her shoulder. She was trying to make it easy on him and was being very obvious, but he apparently was a bit of a blockhead because he stared at her in confusion. She couldn't help but roll her eyes.

She then walked back towards him, once more gripped his jacket in her teeth, and then tugged him forward a few steps. She turned around again and began walking back the way she had come. This time, she heard him make a small sound of understanding, and he began to follow her.

She nodded once to herself and walked through the forest back home to Kate's cottage.

When they reached the cottage, Whisper let out a short bark to announce their presence.

The little boy nearly jumped out of his skin at the sound. Then he laughed nervously in embarrassment.

At the sound, Kate came outside. She knew that Whisper only made noise when something important was going on. Since it was now early November, she had also wisely grabbed her blue cloak before leaving the cottage. And, like always, when she wore it, she had pulled the hood up to cover her face. You never knew who might come calling in the middle of the forest, after all.

As Kate exited the cottage, she saw the boy and, Whisper could tell, was pleased that she had thought to help him with whatever it was that was troubling him. She held out a hand and beckoned him closer, but he stayed stock still, staring at her. She shook her head and looked at Whisper.

The wolf nodded and then once more took the boy's jacket in her teeth gently and pulled him forward. He planted his feet at first, but she was persistent and much bigger than he was, and eventually, he took a few halting steps closer to Kate.

Kate knelt in a welcoming gesture and said, "It's all right. I want to try to help you."

The boy mumbled something that she couldn't quite hear.

"I'm sorry, but what was that?" She asked.

Whisper let go of his jacket, and he stopped walking. He scuffed his feet in the dirt as he looked down. "It's just that, ma'am, everyone's always warned me about you."

She tilted her head and asked softly, "What exactly do they say?"

He glanced up shyly through his long black lashes. "Well, ma'am . . . it's just that . . . everyone says that you're a . . . a . . . " and then he mumbled the last word again.

She chuckled and helped him out. "A witch? Is that it?"

He nodded and continued to stare at the ground.

"It's true, I am a witch." She said quietly.

He looked up in alarm, with wide, terrified eyes, and Whisper felt certain that he would either faint from sheer nerves or else bolt like a rabbit for home.

Kate chuckled again and stood up, offering him her hand. "While I may be a witch, I can assure you that I've never turned anyone into a toad, I don't ride a broomstick at night, and I've never eaten any children."

He made a gulping sound, and she laughed. "I'm teasing you; it's all right, honestly. Come inside. I can fix you something to eat, and then maybe I can help you with whatever is troubling you."

He didn't take her hand, so she moved to the doorway of the little cottage. Once there, she turned and looked back at him. His knees were now audibly knocking together in fear. She shrugged and then went inside without him.

After a few moments, she came back outside with a cup of steaming tea in her hands. But she didn't hand it to the boy. Instead, she took a long sip and sighed with contentment. Then she reached into a pocket and withdrew a small piece of candy. This she handed to him.

He took it with shaking fingers and nodded his thanks. As he greedily began to unwrap it and eat it, she said mildly, "And if I had wanted to hex you, I wouldn't have let you enter my woods."

He looked up in alarm, and she laughed, "Everyone always seems to think the worst of me, yet all I've ever done is try to help them."

She took another long sip of tea and then nodded toward the cottage. "Want to come inside now?"

He looked behind him and all around outside until, finally, he nodded slowly and began to walk forward toward the cottage. He had nowhere else to go.

TWELVE

All three of them walked inside, and Kate pulled a chair out at the table for the boy. He sat and heaved a sigh. Kate took a seat at the other end of the table, opposite him, to give him some space.

"Now, then, why don't we start with the basics and the easy stuff? I am Kate. And that is Whisper." She pointed at the wolf. "What's your name?" She asked.

He took a deep breath to steady his shaking hands and then looked her in the eyes. "My name is Pinolo."

"All right, Pinolo, why don't you tell us what's the matter? We want to help." Kate said. As he sat there across from her, she took in his appearance, and her curiosity was peaked. Pinolo was not actually a boy but, rather, what appeared to be a wooden toy. He seemed so lifelike and real that she doubted most people could even tell the difference.

When Kate realized this, she covered up her astonishment by taking another sip of her tea. The boy, who had not begun to tell his story yet, was staring at the table, not meeting her eyes. This gave her a few moments to really study him.

The details on him were exquisite; he was masterfully carved from pine, and even the lines from the tree that had made him matched his arms and legs where veins would be in a human boy. His clothes were real, though, hanging off of his skinny arms and legs.

His face was the most detailed of all. She could see that the top of his head, under his silly-looking pointed hat, was painted black on top to make it look like he had hair on his wooden head. He had rosy cheeks, and his eyes and lips were so lifelike that Kate had to try not to stare at the simple beauty of the elegant crafting. Someone very skilled had taken the time and put in the effort to create a stunning and extremely lifelike piece of art.

The one flaw she could find, and she was by no means an expert woodcarver, was that his nose seemed . . . off. It was centered on his little face, but it was peg-shaped and didn't seem to match the rest of his artfully crafted body, almost like it had been an afterthought on the woodcarver's part.

She took all this in and reminded herself that everyone had their problems and that she should not judge. She had been wrongfully accused, and people judged her all the time because of what she was and how she looked. She smiled to herself and nodded at him.

"Please, Pinolo, tell me what's wrong?"

He took a deep breath and began to talk, slowly at first, but he gathered speed as he went along. "As you can see," He gestured down at himself with pride, "I am a wooden boy." Kate nodded, and he continued, taking a deep breath. "My father, Geppetto, is a wonderful craftsman. He made me all by himself!"

Kate smiled and then reminded herself that he couldn't see it. As much as she would prefer to take off her cloak inside her own home, she knew that her face would startle the child into not speaking at all. So she sat with her hood up and her face hidden.

"Go on, child." She said, gesturing with a hand.

He smiled proudly, and his little chest swelled as he continued. "I am the first of his creations to be given life because I'm so authentic! Once my father completed making me, he wished so hard that I would become a real boy so he wouldn't be alone anymore that a fairy answered his wish and made me alive.

"My father was so overjoyed at the fairy's gift that he wanted to show me off as the son he had always longed for, and so we left home to go to a local fair. But along the way, I wandered off into the forest and got lost. That was several days ago. And now I cannot find my father!" At that last, the little boy burst into tears all over again. He put his face in his hands and shook his head back and forth as he sobbed.

"There, there, Pinolo, please don't cry," Kate said. She walked over and knelt beside his chair while Whisper watched from the floor.

He snuffled and snorted and finally looked up at her through his watery eyes.

"I can help you find your father." She said, patting his knee.

Pinolo smiled weakly and said, "Oh, thank you, ma'am!" He wrapped his arms around her neck and hugged her tightly.

Suddenly, he gasped, "Oh no!"

Kate sat back and held him at arm's length, confused. Before her very eyes, as Pinolo watched too, cross-eyed, his little peg nose suddenly quivered and began to grow. Kate felt her eyes widen; sometimes, the creatures that came to her for help were very strange indeed.

The nose didn't grow for long, but it was definitely longer than it had been a moment before. Pinolo released her and touched it gingerly. Then, he burst into fresh tears.

Kate got up and went to the pot hanging over the fire. She mumbled a few words as she crushed some herbs into the pot. Then, she poured the contents into a small bowl and offered it to the boy. He drank it thirstily and then wiped a hand across his mouth.

"That should help calm you. Now, tell me, why did your nose grow?" Kate sat back down across from him.

Pinolo stared at the table. He mumbled something and sniffled.

"I'm sorry, but I did not hear that," Kate said.

He heaved a great sigh as if the weight of the world itself was on his small shoulders. "My nose grows when I lie." He mumbled.

Kate brought a hand up to cover her mouth as she tried not to giggle: strange creatures indeed.

"What exactly did you just lie about?"

"I told you that I got lost. I didn't get lost; I ran away." He said.

Kate's eyebrows furrowed. "But you said you loved your father and that you were both happy. Why would you want to run away from that?"

He sighed again. "I want to see the world! And he's an old man, so how could he travel with me since I am young and full of energy?"

Kate sat back in her chair and crossed her arms in front of her. "Then why are you so upset now? You've got your freedom."

"I made a huge mistake! The world is a terrifying place! And now I want to go home." He glanced down at his nose as if out of habit, but it remained normal.

Kate raised an eyebrow. "Why are you looking at your nose? Did you just tell a lie?"

Pinolo shook his head. "Not exactly."

"Go on," Kate said.

"I've been away from father for a few days now. And I've come to realize that the world is full of all sorts of things. Things that are good or bad. Or both." He took a deep breath. "And some things that are pure evil. I'm scared of those sorts of things."

Kate nodded. "I agree. That's why it's always best to try to protect yourself if you can. And to stay close to those who love you. They can help protect you. Your father would protect you, I'm sure."

Pinolo nodded and said softly. "I know that now. But those evil things are still out there . . . trying to get me."

Kate narrowed her eyes. "What do you think is after you? And how do you know? Did something attack you?"

The little boy wrapped his arms around himself. "The first day after I ran away from Father, I came across a woodsman in the forest. He was chopping a tree down with a large silver axe. But I was polite to him." He hurried to add. "Despite my politeness, when he saw me, he came towards me with his axe. He did not look friendly. And he said, 'You are an abomination and cannot be allowed to live.'" The little boy began to shake slightly as he remembered.

Kate made a soothing sound and then asked quietly, "What did this woodsman look like?"

"He was tall and strong-looking in green and brown hunting leathers. He had a huge, bushy black beard and wore a large furry hat that almost covered his eyes. His black eyes looked mean."

Kate gasped, and Pinolo's eyes looked at her sharply. "Do you know this scary man?"

She nodded slowly. "Aye, unfortunately, I do." She glanced at Whisper, who was now looking at her intently, too.

"Why have you not spoken of him before now?" The wolf asked in her mind.

Kate ignored her for a moment and concentrated on the boy. "If this man is who I think he is, you were right to run for your life. He is very dangerous."

"Can he find me?" The boy whispered.

Kate glanced towards the door and then shook her head. "Not if I put a spell of protection around you."

Pinolo seemed uneasy at that. "But isn't magic evil too?"

Kate smiled ruefully. "No, not all magic is evil. It's the intent that makes it so. Since this is intended to protect you and not harm you, it's considered safe and good magic."

The little boy nodded at that and sat back in the chair, his feet dangling off the floor.

"How can you do this?"

Kate stood up and walked over to one of the shelves in her kitchen. She looked at the various jars there and then finally selected a few before bringing them back to the table. She opened them and took out various amounts of the substances in them, laying them across the table as the boy watched.

"I will help you, but you must do as I say. Following my instructions is very important. If you don't, the spell could go wrong. All right?" She began cutting items and then putting them all in a large bowl together.

Pinolo nodded and watched her, fascinated.

She glanced at him, and he nodded again and said, "Yes, I promise!"

Satisfied that he would obey her, she went back to preparing the spell. She moved to the fireplace, took some of the ashes out, and mixed those in, too. She also grabbed a few candles and a small knife. Then she went to a cupboard and, after rummaging inside for a few moments, exclaimed, "Aha!"

Whisper tilted her head.

Kate returned to the table and lit the candles. Then she said a few quiet words over the bowl, motioning with her hands, which were outstretched over it. She took up whatever it was she had taken from the cupboard and held it tightly in her right hand over the bowl. She murmured words again and then dipped it into the bowl. There was no light this time, unlike the previous spell Kate had performed in front of Whisper, nor any frothing blue stuff that ran onto the floor.

After a few moments of silence, as Pinolo and Whisper looked on in wonder, Kate smiled and brought her hands down again.

She walked over to Pinolo and knelt by his chair. She opened her hand, and resting in her palm was nothing but a small, round pendant. There was a strange symbol drawn on it that was pulsing with a faint orange glow. The little boy stared at it wide-eyed.

Kate moved to place the pendant around his neck. He let her and didn't say a word, all the while watching what she was doing.

When she was finished, Kate walked over to her chair by the fire and sat down, exhausted.

"There, that will protect you now. As long as you don't take it off." She said.

Pinolo jumped up from his chair and scampered over to hug her. "Oh, thank you!

She refrained from hugging him back, though. "I will help you find your father. But you must stay the night since it is growing dark and I'm now very tired. We'll set out first thing in the morning. All right?"

He nodded emphatically, and she continued, "Because I've helped you, you must promise never to run away from your troubles again."

Pinolo looked skeptical, so she added, "Remember that I'm a witch, so I can hex you into doing it anyway. It just doesn't taste bad if you agree on your own."

Whisper's head snapped up, and she looked at Kate. They both knew that there was no way Kate could hex anyone into doing something they didn't want to do. Kate made a motion with her hand, dismissing Whisper's look. The wolf huffed and put her head back down.

The little boy was unaware of this, and so he nodded his head at Kate. "Aye, I promise."

After a few moments, Kate patted his back, and the little boy released his firm hold. She then stood up and walked over to her bed. She pulled a blanket off of it and prepared a small bed by the fire for Pinolo. When she was finished, she motioned for him to lie down, which he did gratefully.

"In the morning, we'll find your father," she said. She turned and walked over to her bed and, after preparing for sleep, got under the covers.

Whisper quietly padded over towards Kate, and the wolf flicked her ears once in the direction of the boy. He was sleeping peacefully, so she lay down to sleep on the floor beside Kate's bed.

THIRTEEN

Just before dawn, as per usual, Kate rose and dressed and then went outside to take care of her chickens. Whisper walked along silently behind her. As she turned to close the latch to the chicken coop behind her, Kate jumped at seeing Whisper sitting in the grass on the other side, watching her.

"I didn't hear you come with me this morning."

Whisper bowed her head, a sign of apology for her startling Kate.

Kate resumed what she was doing, but she heard in her mind, "Are you going to tell me how you know him?"

Kate shrugged. "He's someone from my past."

Whisper sighed. "You've told me before that we cannot escape our past. It's why you still think you can help me remember mine."

"That's true. Except, in this case, it's safer for all of us to forget about my past."

Whisper made a low whimpering sound in her throat.

Kate looked up sharply and glared at the wolf. "Just drop it, all right?"

Whisper tucked her tail between her legs and lay down in the grass, her head between her paws. "Someday, I may remember my past. And if I do, I hope you'll share whatever secrets you're hiding about your own." But Kate dutifully ignored her.

Once the chores were finished, the two of them went back inside the little cottage. Pinolo had awoken while they were outside, and he had taken it upon himself to tidy up inside. He had cleaned up his sleeping area and wiped the table, and he was sweeping the floor when they came back inside.

"What a pleasant surprise! Thank you, Pinolo." Kate said, patting the little boy on the shoulder. He beamed at her.

She then prepared a light breakfast for them all. Once everything was back in its place, she packed some provisions in a knapsack, and the three of them set out.

Whisper led them through the trees and down the well-worn path towards the main road, which was several miles off. It was a cart trail that led through the heart of the forest, and it would be easier going once they reached it. For now, there were bumps and tufts of grass across their path, so their progress was slower. The main road would take them either east, towards the coast, or west, towards the small town of Thuaid. They would head towards the town. However, Whisper would have to leave them before reaching the town, as even a well-behaved wolf in town would cause a panic.

It was shortly after midday, and they were still on the rough forest trail. In some places, they even had to wade through waist-high under-brush. Pinolo and Kate kept sight of Whisper only through the rustling of the brush before them.

The wolf had just disappeared again around a bend in the trail when Kate and Pinolo heard a loud snapping sound followed by a shrill yelp. Kate rushed forward into an extremely dense section of the trail. Whisper was lying in the grass on her side, whining softly over and over again. Her right front paw was caught in a metal trap that had been cleverly hidden in the weeds.

Kate felt her eyes widen in horror, and the color drained from her face. There was so much blood that, at first, Kate thought Whisper's paw had been completely severed. But upon closer examination, she found that the trap had only bitten deeply into the wolf's lower foreleg.

Using a heavy stick, Kate pried the jaws of the trap open while Pinolo removed Whisper's leg from it. The metal contraption snapped shut the moment Kate let go of the stick.

They all jumped at the awful sound.

Kate turned to begin administering to Whisper when the wolf's eyes rolled up into her head, and she suddenly began to thrash and shake. Kate held a hand in front of Pinolo to keep him away. She knew instinctively that they shouldn't touch the wolf while she was like this.

Then Kate heard in her mind, "*Help us! Please! Don't let that thing get me! Grandma, watch out! Nooooooo!*"

Her eyes widened, and she put a hand to her heart. Was Whisper remembering something from her past?

The wolf's voice continued in her mind, but this time, it took on a pleading and pathetic quality. "*He's here for me. I don't want to go. Mama, Papa, nooooo! Help me!!!*" The last words ended in a high, lupine-wailing howl. Then she lay still. So still that Kate held her breath, fearing that her friend had abruptly died. But then, Whisper took a ragged breath and raised her head.

"What happened?" She asked.

Kate reached out a hand and laid it on Whisper's flank to try and calm her. "You accidentally stepped on a hunting trap. We freed your leg, but I need to bind it to stop the bleeding and ward off infection. Please try to hold still."

The wolf nodded and laid her head back down in the grass, closing her eyes.

Kate reached into her rucksack and pulled out a strip of cloth and a small pouch of herbs. She crushed the herbs and added some water to create a paste, which she then smeared onto the cloth. She wrapped that around Whisper's leg firmly.

Once she was finished, she patted Whisper and said, "I doubt you can walk, so we're going to fashion a travois for you. Just rest; it won't take us long."

Kate then turned to Pinolo. "Please go into the trees and find us some sturdy branches with leaves still on them, if you can. We will tie them together so we can drag Whisper along with us." As he moved to obey, she called after him, "But don't stray too far off the path. Stay within shouting distance, all right?"

He looked over his shoulder, a determined expression on his wooden face, and nodded once, firmly.

While he was gone, Kate set about cutting some young-growth trees into long poles. She used a knife she also had in her rucksack, and once the small trees were felled, she made sure there were no branches or leaves on them. Then, she lashed all three together, forming a crude triangle.

Pinolo came back, dragging several large branches behind him. They were from pine trees so that they would make for a softer bed for Whisper. He dropped them at Kate's feet and smiled proudly. She nodded her appreciation at him and began laying them across her triangle. Once she was finished, she straightened her hood and said to the boy, "Now we have to move her onto it so we can travel again. But we have to be careful because she's in pain. Let's do it slowly, all right?"

He moved around to Whisper's back legs and patted her firmly in reassurance. "We'll try not to hurt you, Whisper." Her tail thumped once in acknowledgment.

"On three: one, two, three, heave," Kate said, grasping Whisper's front legs and, as gently as she could, hoisting the wolf onto the travois. With a little bit of wiggling and pulling, they both managed to secure the wolf. Whisper patiently never made a sound as she was pulled and prodded.

When they were finished, Pinolo wiped a hand across his wooden forehead. "That was hard, but I'm glad we helped her."

Kate smiled in spite of herself. "Helping others is easy; it's *not* helping them when they need it that's hard."

She glanced up at the sky; it was now late afternoon. "We need to hurry, though and get to the main road before it gets dark. Once there, it's not a long walk out into the fields."

Kate took up one of the poles and Pinolo the other, and, with a bit of effort, they managed to get the sled moving. Thankfully, it wasn't long before they broke free of the dense underbrush, too, which was a good thing, considering how slow their progress had been even before Whisper had been hurt.

When they reached the main road, they began to head west towards Thuaid, the nearest town. Eventually, the trees began to thin, and they could tell that the sun was beginning to set. As they finally reached the edge of the forest, both Kate and Pinolo put their poles down and paused to rest. They were both exhausted since Whisper was not a normal-sized wolf.

Kate offered the boy some water, which he took and drank thirstily. When he was done, she finished off the last of it herself, tilting the canteen back as her other hand kept a firm hold on her hood.

When they had rested for a few moments, Kate said, "We need to hide Whisper here; she cannot go with us into Thuaid."

They pulled the wolf's sled off into the underbrush, and Kate covered her with ferns to keep her warm. "We're going into the town; it's not far off. We'll likely spend the night at an inn, and then I'll come back to check on you in the morning." She glanced at the sky. "You should be warm and dry as it shouldn't rain tonight." The wolf whimpered softly. "I promise I'll come back for you. You'll be safe here, and I'll make sure to bring you a big breakfast."

She then reached into her rucksack and withdrew the last of their provisions, a chunk of bread and some cheese. She laid it down by Whisper, who sniffed at it dubiously. "I know it's not what you're used to, but it will tide you over until the morning. I'll be back, I promise."

She scratched the wolf behind her torn ear and then stood up and began following the path toward Thuaid. She could see curls of chimney smoke rising only a few hills away. If they kept moving, they'd easily reach it before full dark.

"Come on, Pinolo, we still have a little farther to go." They walked down the path and didn't look back.

Once they were out of sight, Whisper gobbled up the food hungrily. Then she sighed. It would be hard to pass the night here, alone, in the woods. But she was a wolf, after all, and the woods were supposed to be home to her.

She laid her head back down and closed her eyes. Her right paw burned with a painful fire, even though Kate's poultice had dulled it at first. She wondered if she would ever stop getting injured through no fault of her own.

As she drifted off to sleep, she wondered who could have set the metal trap there in the first place. It wasn't a commonly used path, and, as far as she knew, not many people even knew the path existed. Most either took an old path to Kate's cottage or else ended up nearby through sheer dumb luck. It would have been a real tragedy if some human had stepped on the trap instead or, even worse if a child had gotten hurt. Those sorts of traps were meant for four-legged predators, and because human bones were so fragile, a human leg might have been snapped clean off.

Whisper shuddered at that thought, but then she slowly drifted off to sleep. The last thing she remembered was hearing the sound of an owl hooting overhead.

FOURTEEN

She woke to birdsong overhead and realized she was shivering. Raising her head, she saw that the sun had risen high in the sky, and it was now early afternoon. Whisper gingerly stood up and shook herself all over, getting rid of the tree branches which had covered her. Taking a deep breath, she enjoyed the fresh scent of pine needles and the damp earth smell of the woods.

She slowly stretched and was relieved to see that Kate's bandage had not come off during the night. Her leg felt a bit better; it wasn't burning anymore, though it did ache, and Whisper knew she would have to take it easy for a while again.

She was just trying to decide what she was going to do since she was ravenously hungry when she heard the sound of footsteps coming down the path towards her. She ducked into the underbrush to hide; people did not like wolves, and she didn't want to startle someone who might hurt her.

As she waited, the sound grew louder, and she realized that it was actually two pairs of footsteps: one lighter, which she recognized as Kate's now, and the other a heavy stomping accompanied by a clopping sound. She realized the latter must be a horse.

She heard Kate call out, "Whisper, I'm back. You can come out of hiding now."

The wolf gingerly walked out onto the path, limping with her hurt paw. "And I brought you some easier transport, too."

Whisper eyed the horse dubiously. The horse stared back at her placidly. He was large, even for his breed, and seemed to tower over Kate. Long blonde hair covered most of his thick hooves, and his pale, cream-colored mane fell into his eyes. He had a bobbed tail, and he was wearing a heavy harness.

He whickered at her, and she tilted her head to the side. "Kate, why did you buy a horse?"

Kate smiled and patted the horse's flank. "I can't drag you back home all by myself. Besides, we could use him to plow a field. Then we can grow different types of foods, and we won't have such meager helpings all winter long. Plus, I got him at a great bargain."

The horse neighed and nodded his head. "You're right, I did," Kate said, smiling. The wolf eyed them both skeptically.

"When Pinolo and I reached the inn last night, we had dinner . . ." She began, but Whisper's stomach growled at the mention of food, so she stopped and reached into her rucksack. She brought out a nice steak and laid it down in front of the wolf, who immediately devoured it.

"Thank you," came the wolf's words to Kate's mind.

Kate nodded and continued, "After dinner, he went to sleep, but I stayed up for a bit and made some inquiries. I asked around and found out that Geppetto had been looking for Pinolo, too. He had just left the inn before we got there! So, early this morning, we followed where he went and caught up to him just before lunch. Pinolo was very happy to see his father again. And Geppetto was so excited to have his beloved son returned to him that he paid me a few coins for my trouble of bringing them together again." She shrugged. "I didn't expect payment for it, though; doing good deeds is something I enjoy, but the old man wouldn't take no for an answer, so I accepted the coins as graciously as I could and then went back to town and bought Herman here." She patted the horse again, who whinnied.

Whisper listened to all of this as she licked her lips. She was still a bit hungry, but the steak had helped.

"Now we can get you back home easily, too," Kate said. "I'll simply attach the travois to Herman, and we can head for home."

She attached the poles, and then all three of them began the long walk back home.

Herman seemed to take to Whisper amicably enough; her being a wolf didn't seem to bother him even a little bit. Of course, that could simply have been because he was so large, and any wolf, magical or not, would be a fool to try and mess with him.

As they walked, with Whisper being dragged behind Herman and the horse dutifully following Kate, the wolf began to drift off to sleep once more.

Before she knew it, Kate was detaching the harness and travois and was leading Herman around the back of their little cottage. Whisper could hear the witch talking to him as she got him settled.

They didn't have a barn, but there was a small three-sided building with an open front. It was shabby, but at least it would keep the horse dry for the time being. Kate usually stored her few tools out there. It was also where she could butcher a chicken for food without any of the other chickens seeing.

Whisper heard her finish and then saw her walk back around to the front of the cottage.

"He's all settled in; now, let's get you inside so I can put a fresh dressing on your paw."

Whisper nodded and heaved herself to her paws. She limped inside and lay down by the fireplace. Then she watched as Kate prepared a new poultice, which she then applied to a fresh bandage.

She gently unwrapped the old one, and as she was putting the new one in place, Whisper asked her something that she had been thinking about. "Why do you suppose that trap was out there in the first place?"

Kate glanced at her but continued working. "I don't know."

Whisper sniffed. "I think you do. Has someone been doing that around here often?"

Kate stopped what she was doing and looked the wolf deeply in her hazel eyes. "Not often, but occasionally, I'll find something like that. It's not too close to here, but it's close enough that I think someone's trying to watch me and is being very cautious about it."

Whisper tilted her head. "Who would want to hurt you?"

Kate finished wrapping the bandage and then sat down in her rocking chair as she stoked the fire. "Lots of people, I suppose." Her eyes grew distant, and Whisper moved to place her head in the woman's lap.

"But you're thinking of someone specific, aren't you?"

Kate idly petted her head and nodded. "Aye, and he's not a nice man. Not a nice man at all." Her words held the heat of anger but also a hint of sadness and regret.

"Is he the one who did that to your face?" Whisper asked gently. They had never spoken about it before, but Whisper had always wondered.

Kate stared into the fire as it crackled and popped. "No, not directly at least. But he is the reason behind why they did it."

"Why, *who* did it?"

Kate sighed. "Some of the townsfolk."

Whisper's head snapped up in alarm. "You mean the people you are always trying to help did this to you?"

She nodded. "They usually mean well, but magic scares them badly. They were afraid, and it . . . got out of control too quickly."

Whisper shook her head. "And yet you still help them?"

"When I can, aye, because it's the right thing to do." Kate shrugged.

Whisper laid her head back down in her lap. "You don't have to tell me about it if you don't want to."

Kate resumed petting her. "It's all right if we're going to keep being roommates; you should know some of my past. It's important, much as I'd prefer to forget about it. And maybe something about my story will help jog your memory."

FIFTEEN

Kate settled deeper into the rocking chair. And she was quiet for a long time, so much so that Whisper thought she wasn't going to speak again. But then she spoke softly, "It happened a few years ago. I wasn't living here alone, though; I had a . . . lover.

"As a witch, I had been living out here alone. One day, he came walking down the path and found my cottage by accident, he said. We became lovers, but those sorts of relationships were frowned upon in Thuaid. He eventually started to stay here with me. It was pleasant, a sort of uncommon marriage arrangement, which we were both happy with.

"He'd go out in the mornings and take care of his foresting business, and then he'd come back after sunset. We'd have dinner together and then enjoy each other's company. He didn't seem to mind that I was a witch, and even though his business sometimes required that he was gone for several nights at a time, our simple life together was perfect."

Kate paused and gazed down at her stomach. "Then I found out I was with child. A happy accident, which we were both excited over."

She stopped talking then, and Whisper looked up. There were tears in her eyes, but she rubbed a hand across them haphazardly. The wolf nudged her other hand with her cold nose and thumped her tail on the floor once in encouragement to continue.

Kate took a deep breath and closed her eyes, "I lost the baby." It came out barely above a murmur.

She took a shuddering breath and then opened her eyes to stare into the fire once more. "I lost the baby, and it caused a rift between us.

Although he didn't say it outright, I knew he blamed me for losing the baby. And he wasn't just upset or frustrated; he was angry about it.

"It was then that I began to see the sort of man he really was. I guess my love for him blinded me because I didn't see that he was really cruel and heartless. I saw it once with my own eyes when he went out to kill a chicken for our dinner. He was outside, and I followed shortly thereafter to ask him something. I walked towards the chicken coop, and I don't think he knew I was there because I heard one of the chickens make a strangled sort of sound. I crept around the side of the coop and saw him pulling its feathers out as he had it hanging from a wire. The noose wasn't tight enough to kill it, but it was slowly suffocating. He had a sick sort of smile on his face as he did it, too, eyes glazed over and staring straight at that poor chicken. But I went back inside the cottage and didn't confront him.

"And another time, he actually hit me. I hadn't been paying enough attention to some bread baking, so I burnt it. He got mad because I had been careless, so he hit me." She shrugged.

She then wrapped her arms around herself. "After he hit me, I swore to myself that if he ever raised a finger to hurt me again, I would make him pay for it. At this point, I wanted him to leave me alone. I would have been content if he'd gone out on business and never come back. But I guess I'm the one who paid in the end.

"It was only a few days later when I did something else that angered him. I don't remember what exactly it was; a lot of what comes next is a blur to me, but he raised a fist to hit me across the face. I raised my hand and pointed my finger at him, looking like I was about to hex him. His face went white, and he stepped away from me. I don't think I would have been able to hurt him, but my actions were enough. He stared at me with his mouth hanging open in shock. Then, he grabbed his things and ran out of the house screaming, 'You're going to regret this, witch!' I had hoped that was the last I was going to see of him.

"I had thought he would simply leave me alone. But I was wrong because he incited the village against me. The next night, I heard people yelling as they tramped through the forest, coming towards my cottage. I rarely receive visitors here, and when I do, they never come in groups, always alone or, in only a few cases, with one other person. So, I was alarmed that a large-sounding group was approaching. I didn't think most of the villagers knew where I lived anyway."

Kate took a deep breath, and her voice began to shake slightly, "When they came for me, they were yelling and angry. But as soon as they were just outside, they stopped, and everything was deadly quiet. He came forward and ordered me to come out. I didn't think I had much to fear from the villagers; I had helped some of them, and I wanted to try to calm them so that they would go home. I walked outside. I should have just stayed inside and bolted the door.

"They had formed a semicircle around my cottage, and he was standing before them with a torch in his hand. Some of the others had torches, too, but a few had pitchforks and shovels. They all looked so angry, and I still cannot understand why.

"When I came outside, he pointed a finger at me and shouted: 'You're a witch, and so you must be purged for your crimes!' I remember him striding forward and grabbing me. I was so surprised that I don't think I fought back. He grabbed me by my neck and forced me to walk out in front of him. Then someone in the crowd tossed him a rope, and he put it around my neck."

She put a hand to her throat as if remembering the feel of the noose around her neck. "He tightened it, but not enough to strangle me. Then he dragged me over to the trees and strung the rope up." She shuddered, and Whisper whimpered. "I thought they were going to hang me. And at that point, since I had already lost the man I loved and the baby, I didn't care if I lived or died, so I didn't struggle. But they had a worse fate in mind for me, one his cruel mind devised especially for me.

"Once the rope was angled over a tall branch, he tied my hands behind my back. Perhaps to make me extra secure, or perhaps so I couldn't use my magic; I'm not sure. But then he took hold of the end of the rope while a few of the villagers brought over their torches.

"They placed them on the ground in front of me and rejoined the others. He then put one of his booted feet against my back, and so I naturally had to lean forward. I thought I was going to fall forward into the flames while being slowly strangled, but when the rope went taught, I was merely suspended over the fire."

Tears began to trickle down Kate's face, but this time, she didn't move to brush them away.

"As I hung over the fire, with the rope biting into my neck, which wasn't tight enough to choke me to death, the fire licked upwards and caught my hair. My hair burned. And once the fire was finished with my hair, it started on my face." She reached up and traced her fingers lightly over her burn scars.

"I don't remember much after that. Only after what seemed like an eternity of agony as my face burned I was lowered to the ground and untied. He kicked me once, which drove the air from my lungs. Before he stomped off, he put his face close to mine and whispered, 'If I had had my way, witch, you would have burned completely. They only wanted to teach you a lesson. I wanted you to die, slowly and painfully.' Then he spat in my face before walking away. I haven't seen him since.

"As I lay there in pain, I was dimly aware of the villagers leaving. I heard murmurs of apology and quiet sounds of regret, but no one stayed to help me. When they were all gone, and I was alone once more, I crawled back inside and tended to my wounds using my herbs and my magic."

Kate looked up then, and there was suddenly a fierce light in her dark brown eyes. "They may have hurt me, humiliated me and maimed me, but I am still here. And," She paused and chuckled, but it held no mirth,

"Some of them still come around asking me for help."

At that, Whisper growled softly. "It's not right that they should seek your aid when they hurt you so!"

Kate shrugged and scratched the wolf's ears. "It is in their nature to hate and fear what they do not understand. It has been that way with witches for centuries. And with other creatures of the forest that do not appear to be friendly. I help them because I should. I would not expect anything else from them. After all, I do not ask that a bee not sting me with its stinger; it's what a bee does; that's in its nature."

"I still do not think it's fair to help those who hurt you," Whisper said.

"What else would I do? I could not find work looking like this," She gestured at her face.

"And there are not a lot of jobs that allow someone to wear a heavy, hooded cloak either. Besides, I'm not particularly skilled at anything that would afford me money anyway. All I know is magic and nature." She shrugged again.

She rose and walked over to the kitchen, and poured herself some water from a pitcher.

"What's more, I don't think I'll ever have to see Jacob Grimm again. Last I heard, he had moved on to another village closer to the coast."

Whisper was strangely silent at that. So the witch glanced at her over her shoulder. The wolf was now sitting up ramrod straight and staring off into space intently. Her eyes had misted over, and they seemed vacant. They were also, oddly, tinged slightly red. Kate could also hear a deep, rolling growl coming from the wolf.

Kate raised her eyebrows in alarm. In the few months she had known her friend, she had never known Whisper to get angry. But the wolf looked absolutely furious now.

She stayed completely still and called softly, "Whisper, are you all right?"

The wolf began to shake and kept up the keening growl deep within her chest. Then she began to snarl and snap her teeth at a seemingly invisible threat. Kate stayed rooted to the spot, afraid to move lest the wolf suddenly attack her and unsure of what else to do.

After several long, strained moments like this, Whisper suddenly shook her head violently and inhaled sharply. She sneezed once and seemed to come back to herself. She looked around the room, dazed, and when her eyes returned to their normal hazel color again, they landed on Kate, and she whined softly.

"What . . . happened?"

Kate stared at her in shock and stayed where she was. "I'm not sure. You seemed to almost go into a sort of trance, but you were still conscious somehow. You were staring off into thin air, and you were growling. The sound was so full of anger and hate. And your eyes . . . they were turning red."

Whisper tucked her tail between her legs and lay down, putting her head on her front paws in shame. "I'm sorry; I didn't mean to scare you. But when you said that name, something just . . . came over me, and I was so full of hate. I saw you, but I also saw him . . ."

Kate cocked her head. "Who?"

The wolf closed her eyes and sighed. "Him. Jacob Grimm . . ." Her eyes suddenly snapped open, and she stared at Kate. "He was the one who hurt you?" Kate nodded slowly. "He seems so familiar . . ."

Kate waited patiently, trying to give Whisper some time to calm down.

The wolf's ears went back as she tried to remember. "What does he look like?"

Kate thought for a moment, "He's tall and has a huge bushy black beard. His beady black eyes miss nothing and are almost hidden behind his stupid furry hat."

Whisper said slowly, "And you said he was cruel and enjoyed inflicting pain on others?"

Kate nodded, and the wolf growled again. "I'm starting to remember. But a lot of it's still fuzzy."

"Take your time." Kate soothed.

"I think he hurt me too. Almost beat me to death." She had closed her eyes, trying to remember.

Kate gasped, and Whisper's eyes opened again. "When I first found you, you had been badly hurt by someone who was brutal." The witch said quietly. The wolf nodded.

"But you had forgotten how you had become so hurt. We had agreed that you would stay here with me since we both knew that there was something else about you, something that sets you apart from wild wolves." Kate said, moving to sit on the floor beside Whisper. She gently petted the wolf, who leaned into her touch for comfort.

"And I had wondered if, in time, you might remember. What else can you remember?"

Whisper huffed out a breath and thought again, this time tilting her head side to side as if sifting through her memories. Finally, she turned and looked at Kate. "He hurt me and wanted to kill me. He wanted to kill me because I am a monster."

Kate shushed her at that, saying, "You're not a monster! You protect and help, and you're certainly the most amiable creature I've ever met. You're more kindhearted and gentler than many of the villagers!"

Whisper's tail wagged once in thanks. "And I remember something else too . . . feeling so sad about something. About loss? I don't know."

Kate patted her shoulder. "Maybe those memories will come back in time too. What else can you remember right now?"

The wolf wrinkled her nose in thought, "I think there was another attack. Besides the one from Jacob, I mean." She squeezed her eyes shut tight. "Yes, I was attacked before. Bitten . . ."

Kate gasped involuntarily, and Whisper opened her eyes. "What is it?" The wolf asked.

"It's just that things that bite, wild creatures, I mean, often transfer their sickness to whomever they attack. If the individual survives, that is. It's almost like a transfer of power. In some cases, it's not actually a sickness, something that can be cured, but rather a specific condition one then has to learn to live with."

The wolf's eyes widened in panic. "And you think because I was bitten by something, I'm now cursed?"

Kate shook her head quickly. "I'm not sure what happened to you. But you're no normal wolf. I mean, look at your size to start with! You're huge, even for a wolf. And when you get angry, your eyes glow red. That's . . . not a good sign." She finished softly.

Whisper put her ears back in worry. "Am I going to turn evil?"

"Things don't just become evil; they consciously make that choice. But in your case, I'm not sure. I'm sorry." Kate moved to stand up and then walked over to the shelf with jars on it. "But I do know how we can figure out what you are for sure." She reached up and drew down a single jar. It contained purple flowers on long stalks. "I think I know, but I want to make sure. Come over here, please."

The wolf obeyed and sat down beside the table as Kate brought out a single flower from the jar. "This is wolfsbane. If you are what I think you are, you should . . ." She never got to finish the sentence because Whisper began to sneeze uncontrollably. The witch nodded slowly. "I was right; you are a werewolf."

SIXTEEN

At those words, Whisper froze, and her eyes widened in horror. She couldn't stop herself from sneezing again, so she looked rather silly, trying to stare in shock with her ears back in fear while sneezing uncontrollably at the same time.

Kate quickly put the wolfsbane back in the jar, and then she fluttered her apron in the air around Whisper to try and clear the air. "Sorry about that," she said.

Whisper's eyes were watering, but she eventually stopped sneezing. Once she did, she walked back over to the fireplace with her tail tucked between her legs and her head hanging low. She laid down and put her muzzle across her paws. "A werewolf? How can this be?" She sounded absolutely dejected, and Kate walked over to sit with her again. She saw that the wolf had begun to cry.

"It'll be all right." Kate soothed her.

"How can it be all right? I'm a monster!" Whisper huffed.

Kate sighed. "It will be all right because we'll *make* it all right. There are worse things in life than being a werewolf."

Whisper picked her head up at that. "Oh? Like what?"

Kate smiled patiently. "Like being dead, for one thing."

Whisper rolled her eyes. "And if I'm a monster?"

Kate shook her head. "I don't think you are a monster. So you're stuck as a werewolf; so what? You've never acted out in violence towards another. And I know you'd never hurt me. How can you be a monster if you'd never actually hurt anyone, hmm?"

The wolf tilted her head in thought. "No, I suppose you're right. But it's not fair."

Kate nodded, "You're right, it's not fair. But then, neither was this." She reached up a hand and gestured towards her face.

Whisper's ears went back in apology, "I'm sorry, I didn't mean . . ."

Kate raised a hand and waved her off.

"It's all right, I knew what you meant. And you're right, it's not fair. But sometimes, that's just the way it is. So we must learn to live with the difficulties and move on." She shrugged. "I haven't let this stop me, so why should being a werewolf stop you from doing what you want with your life?"

Whisper thought about that for a moment and then stopped crying. She sniffled with a wet sound. Then she slowly nodded.

"You're right, of course." She thought again. "And while it's too late to help me, perhaps we can save someone else from ending up the same as we did."

Kate narrowed her eyes. "What do you mean?"

"I mean that we should stop Jacob. He hurt you badly and left you scarred. He nearly beat me to death and left me for dead. He also tried to kill Pinolo, an innocent child. He's a bad man, and he should be stopped." The wolf was on her paws now, and her tail was sticking straight out behind her like a banner.

"What makes you think we're qualified to stop a professional huntsman?" Kate asked.

"You're a witch, capable of magic. And I'm a werewolf . . ." Her eyes glowed with a fierce determination Kate had never seen before.

"Yes, I am a werewolf. And I want revenge."

Kate held up her hands in a gesture of surrender. "Wait a moment. Now you want revenge? That doesn't sound like you at all. We can't just go out, track him and kill him!"

Whisper tilted her head to the side.

"Why not? He's clearly tried to kill us."

Kate sighed. "Because it's simply not *right*, that's why."

Whisper snorted. "Was it right that he maimed you through no fault of your own, and turned an entire village against you? Was it right that he tried to kill me and nearly succeeded? Was it right that he wanted to kill little Pinolo?" Her eyes were wild and roving around now, and she was beginning to growl between her words.

"Whisper, please calm down! I've never seen you get so worked up about something." Kate begged. She remained sitting, though and tried not to agitate her friend any further.

"How can I calm down? I just found out that I'm a werewolf, my family is all dead, and I was almost murdered by a man who likes to hurt my friends!" She snarled. Spittle was now dribbling from her jaws, and her eyes were becoming red-tinged around the edges.

Kate remained rooted to the spot. She wasn't actually afraid that Whisper was going to hurt her, but she had seen wild animals become vicious, and she knew enough to stay where she was and not move.

In sheer frustration, Whisper threw her head back and let out an ear-splitting howl. It reverberated off of the little cottage walls and was then answered by the terrified whinny of Herman and the nervous clucking of chickens outside.

Whisper growled, low and dangerous this time, and then bolted for the door. She couldn't move quickly due to her injured paw, but she was out the door before Kate could even rise from her chair.

She reached for her friend and cried out, "Whisper, come back! Where are you going?"

She was met with silence as the sun began to sink below the horizon. They had talked and worried the day away.

Kate ran to the door and looked out across the trees, but she didn't see the wolf anywhere. She had raced off into the woods.

Feeling at a complete loss, Kate walked out back and tried her best to calm Herman and the chickens. Then she went inside to eat a small dinner and wait. Either Whisper would come back when she was ready, or she would never return. Kate could not possibly track a wolf in the wild that did not want to be found.

She resigned herself to wait.

SEVENTEEN

Whisper had no idea how long she ran; she only knew that she had so much pent-up energy and rage that she had to get away. She knew she would never actually hurt Kate, but she was frustrated and angry and at a complete loss as to what to do with herself. And so she ran.

Trees rushed by her, and their branches snapped at her fur. She leaped over roots and rocks and dodged tree trunks. She splashed through a creek and kept going.

By the time she was gasping for air and felt like collapsing from exhaustion, it was fully dark. She had no idea how far she had run or even in which direction Kate and home now were. She flopped down on the ground and gulped mouthfuls of fresh, crisp air.

She laid her head down on her paws to rest, and she closed her eyes. But this time, no tears of hurt came. She had worn herself out. She huffed and just tried to forget her troubles for a few moments.

The stillness of the dark forest was peaceful. Until, off in the distance, Whisper heard a shrill, high-pitched scream. Her head snapped up, and her ears flicked towards the sound in alarm. It was in a different direction from where she had just run, and it was too high to be Kate's voice. She was on her paws before she even realized she was moving.

Another scream followed at the end of the first, and Whisper found herself running, despite her weariness, towards the sound. She realized, belatedly, that she was, once more, rushing off to help someone else. She locked her teeth together in a grim expression of determination. Kate was right; werewolf or not, she was not evil.

She picked up speed as she followed the fading sound, even as she ignored the pain in her injured paw. The scream did not come again, so Whisper urged her paws to go even faster.

After a few moments, the wolf feared that she had either imagined the sound entirely or else had gotten turned around because she didn't hear anything else. But then, she crashed through a dense glade of trees and saw a huge black shadow of a man towering over the small, shivering and terrified form of a little girl. He had a silver axe in his hand and was just about to bring it down to strike.

Without pausing or thinking, the wolf barreled into the man. She knocked him clean off of his feet, and he went down like a felled tree.

Whisper stood between the man and the little girl, growling deeply in her chest. Her fur bristled around her, and she knew her eyes must be glowing red in anger.

The man lumbered to his feet and bared his teeth at her. It was Jacob Grimm, and he was so angry that he did not appear to recognize her. He brought his axe up to try to kill her.

She dodged aside easily but kept her body between the little girl and him. She put her head down and snarled at him.

He rushed towards her like a bull, head down and axe held before his body. At the last possible moment, she jumped away and grabbed the coat tail of his jacket to spin him around. Her only thought was to keep him away from the little girl. She let go, and he sailed into a nearby tree trunk. She heard a heavy thunk and did not see him move again; he must have been knocked out cold. She snorted; apparently, she wasn't the only one suffering from anger tonight. At least she had been able to control herself, though.

As much as she was tempted to go over and rip his throat out and end this once and for all, the little girl was sobbing and needed to be looked over first. She hesitated, trapped between the desire for revenge and the desire to protect. But after a moment, she snorted again and turned towards the little girl. There would be time enough to finish him later if she so chose.

She walked back towards the little girl and put her ears in a non-threatening posture. She walked closer to the child, wagging her tail slightly. The little girl, who couldn't have been more than eight or nine years old, had her hands up, covering her face. She was sobbing and seemed completely unaware of her surroundings.

When she was close enough, Whisper put her front legs low on the ground while keeping her back legs straight in a pose meant for play. She craned her neck, trying to look up into the little girl's face. She wagged her tail again haphazardly and made a small whimpering sound in the back of her throat.

The little girl looked up, startled, and her bright blue eyes widened in renewed fear. Whisper wagged her tail more quickly and wiggled her back end, trying her best to look gentle and happy. It was a silly move and one that every little child recognizes as a common sign of goodwill and play. The little girl giggled and stopped crying.

Whisper nudged one of the little girl's hands with her cold nose and flicked it up so that her hand was now resting on top of the wolf's head. The little girl automatically started scratching behind one of her ears, and Whisper moaned with pleasure and leaned into it as she kicked one of her paws as if scratching an itch. The little girl scratched harder, so Whisper's paw thumped faster. The little girl laughed in delight.

When she stopped scratching, Whisper leaned against the little girl to offer her comfort. Since she couldn't speak mind-to-mind with her like she could with Kate, actions would have to speak for her. The little girl petted her soft fur and, after a few moments, seemed to compose herself.

She looked into the wolf's hazel eyes and smiled. The gesture lit up her whole face, and even at such a young age, she was breathtakingly beautiful. She had long ebony hair that was cut into bangs that neatly framed her petite, round face. Her blue eyes were wide and bright, and her face was as pure as snow. Her little mouth was heart-shaped, and her lips were as red as blood. However, she did not seem even remotely aware of her beauty.

Whisper was enjoying the attention until she heard Jacob groan from where he was lying. He was waking up, so they had to act quickly. As much as she would prefer to finish him off, she knew that her larger responsibility was to get the little girl to safety. She couldn't protect the girl if she were fighting Jacob again; the little girl might get hurt in the fight instead.

She looked at the little girl and then grabbed her skirt with her teeth, trying to lead her off into the forest. The little girl followed her, but she was slow and tired. They had to move faster before Jacob was aware of his surroundings again.

Whisper crouched down on the ground, looked at the little girl and then over her shoulder at her own back. The little girl caught on quicker than Pinolo had and immediately climbed onto the wolf's back. She clutched Whisper's ruff fur and buried her face in it. The wolf nodded once in satisfaction and then took off running in what she hoped was the direction of home.

After a few moments, she paused in her mad dash. She wanted to put as much distance as she could between them and Jacob. She knew that eventually, the huntsman would wake up and, in a foul temper, he would try to track them. She wanted to be far enough away when he did in order to have time to confuse their trail.

She inhaled deeply and then looked up at the sky. It was coming up to midnight, and the air was cold and crisp. She stared up at the stars and recognized a few of them as pointing in the direction of home. She sniffed the air and caught a faint smell of wood smoke, so she began running again in that direction.

The miles seemed to crawl by this time. When she had been running before, time had seemed to stand still, and she hadn't been aware of exactly how far she had actually run. The return trip was grueling since she was already exhausted.

After several miles, she went out of her way to confuse their trail. She knew Jacob was an accomplished tracker and hunter, and, in his rage, he would likely stop at nothing in trying to find them, so she had to be extremely careful not to lead him straight back to Kate.

She doubled back and retraced her tracks. She crossed streams and scratched at trees. She left tufts of her fur along the trail. She left obvious paw prints in the mud and also more hidden signs like rubbing up against rocks.

It took her hours. All the while, the little girl clung to her back. Eventually, she drifted off to a contented sleep, still clutching tightly to Whisper's fur.

Finally, nearly dropping from her exhaustion, Whisper decided that she had done as well as she could at covering their escape. She sniffed again and then turned towards home. She was coming through the last thicket of trees towards the little cottage when she caught sight of Kate coming outside and looking through the forest. Her friend had a shawl wrapped around her shoulders, and looked like she hadn't slept all night either.

When Whisper entered the small yard in front of the cottage, she wagged her tail briefly at seeing Kate again. Then she nearly fell over from being so tired. Kate rushed forward and helped to ease the little girl off of her back. With her burden lifted, Whisper was able to lurch inside and flop onto the floor beside the fire.

She could barely lift her head as Kate carried the little girl inside and placed her in her bed. The little girl was still fast asleep. Her job done, Whisper nodded once, and then her eyes fluttered closed, and sleep finally claimed her.

EIGHTEEN

She awoke to the sound of slurping. The wolf scrunched her eyes shut tight and whimpered softly. The slurping stopped, and then she felt a warm presence beside her. Someone was petting her fondly with little hands. She opened her eyes and found the little girl hugging her. She thumped her tail against the floor and then looked around for Kate.

The witch was sitting at the other end of the table, quietly eating breakfast. She glanced at the wolf and offered her a small smile. It seemed, at least for the time being, that their discussion from the night before was over.

Whisper glanced out the door; it was morning. Then, her gaze returned to the little girl still wrapped around her. She tilted her head and woofed softly. The sound caused the little girl to look up at her with wide blue eyes. She backed away and then looked over at Kate for reassurance.

Kate smiled and came over to kneel beside them. "This is Whisper, she's my friend." She scratched the wolf's ears affectionately. "She saved you."

Then she looked at Whisper before motioning to the little girl, "And this is?"

"Gweneira." The little girl stood up and curtsied deeply as she answered Kate.

"My full name is Gweneira Harth, but people just call me Gwen." She smiled brightly. "Thank you, Miss Whisper, for saving me."

Whisper nodded once and then looked at Kate again, "She . . . doesn't fear you?"

Kate absently reached up to touch her face, which was uncovered, and smiled, "No, she doesn't seem to be frightened of my scars at all."

Gwen smiled brightly, "Everyone is beautiful!"

Whisper wagged her tail again and then asked Kate, "Did she tell you anything about what happened last night?"

Kate said, "No," and then she answered Gwen's unspoken question as to who she was talking to. "I can hear Whisper speaking in my mind. She asked if you knew what happened last night."

The little girl looked longingly back at the table. "Miss Kate, could I finish my breakfast first, please? I'm really hungry."

Kate nodded, and they went back over to the table and sat down again to finish their food. Gwen slurped her porridge. When she was finished, Kate brought over some food for Whisper and placed the bowl on the floor where the wolf could reach it.

After they were all finished, Kate and Gwen returned to Whisper's side. Kate sat in her rocking chair while the little girl sat on the floor.

"Why don't you tell us what you remember from last night?" Kate asked.

Gwen hesitated and glanced at the wolf. Whisper wagged her tail once in encouragement. The little girl nodded and then sat up straight as if reciting her letters at school.

"My name is Gweneira Harth, and I lost my mother when I was born." She bit her lower lip and blinked rapidly a few times.

Kate looked at Whisper, who tilted her head. The little girl continued, taking in a deep breath as if she were used to repeating this story, even if she didn't completely understand it.

"My mother wished very hard for years to have a baby girl. She wanted it more than anything else in the whole world! One day, when she was sitting and sewing, she looked out her window, and she pricked her finger with her needle. Three drops of blood fell outside on the newly fallen snow. She knew she would have her baby girl but that she would die giving birth to me."

Whisper's ears went back in alarm, and Kate held up a hand, "You don't have to tell us about your entire past; I know it can be painful, just whatever you remember from last night and why the huntsman wanted to hurt you."

Gwen shook her head. "You need to know the beginning if you're going to understand why he was trying to kill me."

Kate raised an eyebrow but then nodded. "Very well; please, go on."

The little girl took another deep breath and then continued as if she hadn't been interrupted. "After I was born and my mother died, my father grew more and more lonely. It was hard raising a baby girl all by himself. But he got married again. And this new woman moved into our home and became my new mother. Daddy told me she was my 'step' mother, but she doesn't like walking up and down steps." She shrugged. "She is very, very beautiful. I think she's the most beautiful person I've ever seen." She sighed, but it held no hint of regret, "But she didn't seem to like me at all.

"She is rich, and when she came to live with Daddy and me, she had servants come too. They helped raise me. They were nice, and I liked them. But she didn't come to see me, even when I was a baby.

"When I was older, I tried to get her to like me; I asked to see her pretty clothes, and I asked about her huge mirror. It seemed like she was always going into her room to look at it. But she often didn't pay any attention to me.

"As I started to grow up, she became even more cold towards me. There was something about me that she didn't like. I have no idea what it is." She furrowed her eyebrows and looked confused.

Kate glanced at Whisper, but the wolf was engaged in the story.

"She knew I liked to go outside, so one day, she did finally talk to me. She told me I was allowed to go outside the castle walls and into the woods if I wished. I thought it was strange that she would suggest something Daddy always told me not to do. But since she was finally nice to me, I went outside. I skipped all the way to the forest!" She smiled brightly. "And she let me go all by myself too, like a big person!

"Once I got out into the woods, I started following a little path. I was happy, so I just walked and walked. I realized I was lost when I got hungry. And then I couldn't find my way home! I was so scared!

"It was after dark, and I was still lost when I stopped by a fallen tree to rest. I didn't think I'd ever get home again. But then I heard soft footsteps behind me. It was the Queen's huntsman; he had found me! I was so glad to see someone I knew that I didn't see his shiny silver axe until he brought it out from behind his back." She shivered before continuing. "He seemed like such a nice man when I had met him before. But his black eyes were mean, and he acted as if he didn't know me. He made me afraid again." She rubbed her arms with her hands as if she were cold.

"I asked if he had come to take me home, but he shook his head. Then he stepped towards me. He was so close that I could see all the fur on his big hat. I didn't like it, so I moved away. He grabbed my wrist and yanked me to my feet; it hurt, and I started to cry. But he ignored me and said, 'I've come to kill you, little girl.'

"I didn't know what to do! He was so big and strong! He let my arm go and then showed me his axe again. He said that the Queen had sent him to do a job, and he intended to do it. He said she wanted me dead and that I had to die because I was so beautiful. She hated that I was more beautiful than she was.

"I begged the huntsman not to kill me. I told him I didn't care how pretty I was. And I told him I was sorry that my stepmother hated me enough to have me killed. He didn't care about my tears or my begging." Gwen closed her eyes briefly before opening them again and taking another, steadying breath. "He said nothing would stop him from doing his job. He said that once he killed me, he would cut out my heart, lungs and liver and take them back to the Queen to prove he'd killed me. Then he smiled, and it wasn't a nice smile either, as he said, 'She is going to eat them to help her devour your beauty.'

"I was too scared to speak! And my legs were shaking so badly that I don't think I could have run away if I tried. I was just so afraid! I closed my eyes tight and prayed that he would at least kill me quickly."

Gwen then looked at Whisper with tears shining in her blue eyes. "But then you came and saved my life. How can I ever thank you?"

Whisper nudged the little girl's hand with her nose, and Gwen began to pet her again. She wagged her tail and then looked up at Kate. "How else can we help her?"

Kate, who had been quiet the entire time Gwen was telling her story, had a strange expression on her face. She almost seemed caught between a good idea and a bad idea, and she seemed a bit confused by the prospect of both. She shook her head slightly, and then her eyes refocused on the wolf at her feet.

Whisper tilted her head to the side. "What were you thinking just now?"

Kate smiled slightly and repeated what the wolf had said in her mind. Then she answered her question, "I was just thinking what a horrible experience that was for such a little girl. I am deeply sorry that you had to go through that, Gwen. Then I was wondering if Gwen would like to stay here with us." She shrugged and then looked at the little girl. "It's a very small cottage, but you don't seem to have anywhere else to go . . ."

Gwen giggled with delight, jumped up and threw her arms around Kate in a fierce hug. "Oh yes, of course! I'd love to stay here with you! Thank you very much!"

Kate beamed and hugged her back. "It's all settled then." She glanced around the small cottage. "Though we may need to move if we keep adding roommates!"

Whisper sighed contentedly. At the sound, Gwen looked over at her and asked, "I saw that you're hurt. May I help you?"

The wolf glanced at Kate. The witch shrugged, so she nodded her head once.

Gwen shuffled over to sit beside her, and then, gently, she took Whisper's injured paw into her small hands. She closed her eyes and breathed deeply for a few moments. After a few moments of this, Whisper tilted her head to the side in confusion.

Gwen began to cry. Not the wracking sobs of sadness or the tears of terror, but simple, pure tears. They splashed onto Whisper's paw, and the wolf instantly felt better. She looked at Gwen in amazement. "How did you do that?" She asked through Kate.

Kate was also staring in shock at what had just occurred. She shook her head slowly. "I don't know how she did that."

The little girl released Whisper's newly healed paw and wiped her eyes. She shrugged.

"I don't know why it happens, but when I think about it and I cry, my tears help to ease the pain."

Whisper licked the little girl's face. "I think we're even now, thank you."

Kate translated for the wolf, and Gwen beamed.

NINETEEN

It was several weeks later, and they had all just turned in for the night. It was well after supper time, and after Kate had read for a while and Whisper and Gwen had played by the fire, all three of them prepared for sleep. They were slowly becoming accustomed to their new routine; each of them had their jobs to attend to, and they all enjoyed spending their free time with each other.

Kate was grateful to have a child finally, and Gwen seemed just as eager to have a mother, someone she had never known.

Despite Whisper still being troubled by her past, the wolf had become comfortable with her new family and routine. She still often wondered what exactly had happened to her, but for the most part, she went about her business as any animal does: with focus and dedication.

They had all settled in to sleep for the night, with Kate in her bed, Gwen nestled beside her on her new makeshift pallet, and Whisper laying at the foot of Kate's bed.

It was after midnight when Whisper's nose twitched in irritation. The wolf sneezed in her sleep, which woke her up.

She immediately sensed that something was wrong. The light from the fireplace cast a flickering, eerie light over the interior of the little cottage, but she could not see anything out of the ordinary. As her eyes focused after being roused from sleep, she sniffed the air, and then her eyes widened in fear. She smelled smoke. And it wasn't coming from the fireplace. She flicked her ears this way and that and caught the sound of crackling tinder from above them; the roof was on fire!

Whisper knew that there was no logical reason that the roof should be on fire, so she jumped to her paws and woke Kate quietly. She gently licked the witch's face, and when she woke up and looked at her, Whisper pointed her nose at the ceiling and whimpered. Kate's eyes were bleary and out of focus, but as soon as she heard the wolf whimper, she was wide awake. She knew that Whisper would never wake her without a very good reason.

"The roof's on fire!" She furrowed her eyebrows at the ceiling. "Why on earth is the roof on fire?" Then she shook her head, "We've got to get out of here, and quickly!" She threw her clothes on as Whisper woke Gwen.

The little girl mumbled something about wanting to sleep longer when Whisper stuck her cold nose right up against her feet. That got her to jump up, fully awake. "Whisper! Why did you wake me?"

Her blue eyes widened in alarm when she saw Kate hurrying around the little cottage.

She coughed and realized she smelled the smoke, too. She jumped out of bed and got dressed as fast as she could. Then she helped Kate grab a few irreplaceable and precious items before all three of them ran out the back door.

Once outside, they could all see the flames licking high into the night sky. The fire was clearly out of control, and there was simply no hope for it. Kate and Gwen watched helplessly as the fire began to trickle down the outside walls of the little cottage.

Meanwhile, Whisper was looking all around because she felt certain that something else was very wrong. Fires didn't just start on roofs; something had to have started it.

The night sky was clear and cold; she could see thousands of stars and the moon in a crescent shape overhead. There were no storm clouds, so lightning was not the culprit. The wolf tilted her head in confusion.

Their fireplace was cleaned out regularly, with Gwen disposing of the ashes behind the chicken coop. The little girl did that chore daily. Besides, even with their little chimney, how could an ember have flown up the flue to land on the thatched roof and ignite? Whisper supposed it was possible, but it just didn't seem at all likely. Likewise, because it was cold, the ember should have snuffed itself out before getting a chance to catch on anything.

Whisper tilted her head the other way and then closed her eyes in concentration. She inhaled deeply, letting the various scents surrounding her envelop her sense of smell completely. There, faintly, once she had sifted and sorted through all manner of other things around her, she caught it. It was vaguely familiar, and it made her hackles rise in anger. It was him, Jacob Grimm.

She growled, and her eyes snapped open. Kate and Gwen were looking at her as if she were mad. "This is no freak accident." She snarled at Kate.

Kate's eyes widened. "Please don't tell me who I think it is that's responsible."

The wolf nodded in confirmation, "Aye, it's him."

Kate ground her teeth and moved away from Gwen. She began to walk around towards the front of the cottage with determined and angry steps. "I've had enough. We're going to take care of him right now."

This time, it was Whisper who pulled her back by grabbing hold of the bottom of her blue cloak. "We can't! He set fire to our home to kill us all. If we let him think he's succeeded, maybe he'll **finally** leave us alone!"

Kate stopped walking and snorted in derision, "You know that's as likely as to have Herman fly around the moon!"

Whisper glanced at Gwen, who was trying to follow the seemingly one-sided conversation without much luck. "If you won't stay away from him for my sake, at least avoid him for hers."

Kate huffed in frustration but then walked back towards them. "You're right, of course." It took her a moment to compose herself before she said, "We need to make sure he thinks we're all dead. Gwen and I will round up Herman and set the chickens loose. Whisper, you sneak around and try to watch Jacob; we need to be sure he thinks we're dead. Don't let him see you." Kate put her hands on her hips, "Can I trust that you're not going to try and kill him yourself?"

The wolf looked affronted. "Of course not; I would rather disappear with you two into the forest. If he really thinks we're all dead, he won't come after us."

She paused and then added with a snarl, "Much as I would like to have the pleasure of killing him myself."

"Whisper, please," Kate begged.

The wolf nodded firmly, "All right, I promise."

Kate sighed in relief, "Thank you. We'll meet you in the forest a few leagues from here, by the freshwater pool. Come on, Gwen, we've got to take care of Herman and the chickens before the fire spreads even more." They both hurried off towards the other animals. Kate glanced back over her shoulder at Whisper once. The wolf nodded again at her. The witch could trust her; much as the wolf hoped for revenge, she would uphold her promise.

She slunk off into the forest and circled so that the burning cottage was now in front of her. She hid in the trees and used the underbrush to mask her presence. Her black fur helped her blend in perfectly with the night and shadows.

She crawled forward on her belly, following the Jacob-smell through the trees until she caught sight of him. He was also hiding among the trees. He was staring fixedly at the door to their cottage, and he had a shotgun raised on his shoulder, ready to fire at the first sign of movement. He had various other weapons, too: a huge machete at his waist, rope slung across his shoulder, a skinning knife on his belt along with wire and some other tools Whisper did not recognize.

He was focused entirely on the cottage. She could, in all likelihood, creep up behind him and bite his neck until he died. The thought made her want to howl in triumph, but she locked her jaws shut tight and remained silent. She had promised Kate. Besides, if she misjudged the distance or if she made any noise, he could turn around in an instant and shoot her. She doubted even Gwen's magical tears could heal bullets.

Whisper narrowed her eyes and waited.

As she lay there in the dark, watching her enemy, who was so close that she could practically taste his sweat, she thought about all the close calls she and her loved ones had had with him. She wanted to growl and snarl but remembered to remain absolutely still and quiet. She watched him breathing slowly and carefully as he watched the doorway.

It would be so easy to sneak up behind him and break his neck with her strong jaws. He wouldn't even make a sound as she would crush his windpipe. Or she could hamstring him and watch him suffer slowly. Her eyes narrowed, and she began to see tinges of red on the edges of her vision. She inhaled deeply and closed her eyes, trying to calm herself. She was shaking with the effort of controlling her anger and need for revenge.

She had to remind herself that if she lost control now, it could very well mean her death. Or, worse yet, the death of her friends who were counting on her to stay silent and watch their foe.

Whisper scrunched her eyes shut tight and concentrated on simply breathing slowly and evenly. After a few strained moments, she felt better, so she opened her eyes. Her ears flicked towards Jacob. She could hear him muttering to himself under his breath.

"Dammit, where are they? They should have run outside by now. If they've burned alive, it'll take all my fun away." He grunted and cocked the hammer back on his shotgun slowly. "All I need is a little teaser of a white shift, or a splash of color of a lock of hair, or a hint of that damned red ribbon the stupid beast wears. Come on, women, where are you all?"

His mumbling became incoherent, but Whisper sensed that he was very frustrated and on edge and, therefore, extremely dangerous. Her ears went back, and she suppressed a growl.

They stayed like that, a man in front and watching the little cottage like a hawk and a wolf close behind him, for what seemed, to Whisper, like hours.

Once the flames had destroyed the entire roof, they started to slink down the outside walls, too. They dribbled down the walls of her home like water.

Eventually, Whisper heard the wooden timbers creaking inside, and the entire thing collapsed in on itself in a shower of sparks, flying embers and crackling flames. She stopped herself from whimpering in despair just in time.

Even after the little cottage collapsed, Jacob remained rooted to his hiding spot, watching intently. There was no sign of movement from inside, and the only sound was the crackling of the slowly dying fire.

He began to grumble again as he lurched to his feet, "Stupid bitches didn't even scream. Where's my satisfaction? At least they're all dead now, and I'm finally rid of all three of them! Not even that witch's magic could have saved them from that inferno, ha!"

He nodded his head once in a jerky motion of completion, and then he spat on the ground towards the cottage. "And good riddance to you monsters!"

Then he stomped off into the woods, never looking back. He passed within a scant few feet from where Whisper lay in the dense underbrush, but he was preoccupied with his completed task and did not see her.

She held her breath anyway and tried not to cringe away from him as he walked by her.

Once his footsteps had faded away into the forest and she was certain she could no longer hear or smell him, she stood up and shook herself vigorously. Her ears flapped against her skull, and she could feel her fur fluffing out again after having laid motionless for hours. Then, she stretched languidly.

When she felt more like herself again, and her limbs were no longer asleep from remaining still for so long, she walked once around the little cottage, eyeing the destruction. Shaking her head in regret, she trotted off into the woods in the direction she knew Kate and Gwen had taken.

It didn't take her long to track them down. She sniffed and then followed Kate's lavender-herb scent into the forest.

When she emerged into a small clearing, Gwen and Kate let out breaths of relief at seeing her. The little girl rushed forward and tackled her in a hug. She scratched Whisper's ears, and so the wolf obliged at the attention and rolled over onto her back, exposing her belly. Kate walked over, and then both of them began tickling her. Whisper wriggled and squirmed but let them have their fun.

Once their simple reunion was over, Kate asked, "So, did you see him?"

The wolf nodded and sat down on her haunches, her tongue lolling out of her mouth. "Aye, and he was so fixated on killing all of us that he never even knew I was there."

Kate nodded and then asked, "What was he doing?"

"He simply watched the cottage burn. He had his gun up and pointed at the doorway. I expect he meant to kill us, one by one, as we fled our burning home." Whisper replied. "He was frustrated that we never seemed to leave, though. He was muttering about wishing us dead and wanting the pleasure of doing it himself." She continued. "I wanted him dead just as badly," Whisper admitted, ducking her head in shame.

Kate moved to scratch her behind her ears. "It's all right. You didn't act on that desire. That makes you better than he is."

Whisper huffed. "Maybe, but he's still alive and can potentially hurt us still."

Kate shook her head, "I don't think so. I think this was the last time he was going to try and kill us. Remember that he thinks we're all well and truly dead this time. He apparently had no idea our home had a back exit. And lucky for us that it did! My magic cannot stop bullets, so one of us, or even all of us, could have been killed had we not run."

Whisper rolled her eyes in a very human-like gesture. "Maybe. But I still think you should have let me kill him."

Kate furrowed her eyebrows, "Now Whisper, that's not right. Just because he has tried to kill us does not give you the right to end his life by your own hands . . . er, teeth and claws."

Whisper put her ears back. "But shouldn't someone do it? He's a vicious and cruel man who delights in causing pain to others. Shouldn't someone take care of him for the betterment of us all? How many other creatures has he killed just for the sake of killing them because they're wild? And how many innocent humans has he killed because they were different?" She looked pointedly at Kate's scarred face.

Kate glared at the wolf and crossed her arms in front of her chest. "Even so, that does not give *you* the right to take his life. Besides, do you really want that on your conscience? Have you ever killed someone before? It may not be as easy as you think."

Whisper looked away from her friend and huffed in frustration. "I don't know. I still think someone should hold him responsible for all that he's done."

Kate knelt on the ground and offered her hand out to the wolf. "In time, someone will. But it doesn't have to be you."

The wolf leaned forward and licked her friend's fingers in acquiescence. "Fair enough."

"I know he has hurt you; I have too . . ." She brought her hand up to trace the scars on her face. "But that doesn't mean we have to be the ones to kill him. We're better than that."

The wolf sighed and then nodded reluctantly. "I suppose you're right. But I'm not happy he's still out there."

Kate stood up and brushed her hands across her apron. "Neither am I, but what else can we do?"

She looked at Gwen and realized that the little girl had no idea what Whisper had been saying. "I'm sorry, Gwen, but Whisper and I were just talking about the Huntsman. I think we've come to a decision, though, on what to do from here." She glanced at the wolf, who nodded, if a bit reluctantly.

"Since we cannot go back to our cottage, we'll have to find a new place to live. We're going to start walking through the forest until we either reach the village or find a good place to start building another home. All right?"

The little girl looked skeptical at first and said, "Do either of you know how to make a house?"

Kate chuckled, "Not exactly. But I'm sure we'll figure something out. These woods are huge; there's got to be someplace we can live."

Gwen shrugged and then took Kate's hand. "Don't you know of anyone who can help us?"

Kate tapped a finger on her lower lip and thought for a long moment. Finally, her eyes widened in recognition. "Yes, of course!"

Whisper stood up, and Gwen smiled. "You've thought of someone who can help us?" The little girl asked.

Kate pretended to be nonchalant. "Maybe I have, and maybe I have not. You two will have to wait and see!"

Whisper tilted her head, and Gwen lifted an eyebrow. "Why the secrets?" She asked.

"Because, like me, his reputation often precedes him, and I don't want you to meet him with any preconceived notions," Kate said.

"What does 'preconceived' mean?" Gwen wrinkled up her little nose.

Kate chuckled, "It means to go in with an already-formed idea of something. He's really a nice man; he's just . . . got a bad reputation." She chuckled again, "And sometimes I think he actually likes it."

She took Gwen's hand again and then picked up a basket Whisper saw that had been sitting on the ground. "What's in there?" The wolf asked.

"The most precious things I could grab before we left the cottage. Plus, a few bits of food for when we get hungry." Kate answered.

Whisper sniffed and caught the faint scent of old bread and a cake or two. She nodded and then said, "All right, lead the way to this mysterious friend of yours."

Kate looked up at the lightening sky for a moment and got her bearings. "He lives near the sea, so we have to head towards the east. And it's going to be a few days' walk from here."

She began walking with Gwen beside her and Whisper trailing behind them. The wolf glanced back over her shoulder towards the remains of their burnt cottage. She wondered if they would be able to start fresh and if their last remaining problem would leave them alone for good this time.

She trotted to catch up to the other two.

TWENTY

That night, once it had grown too dark for the two humans to see to continue walking, they made camp. It wasn't anything fancy, just the bare bones, but all three seemed content enough.

Whisper obviously couldn't start a fire herself, so she went off with Gwen into the woods to help the little girl collect firewood. Kate, meanwhile, started a small fire. When the wolf and the little girl returned, Gwen had a bundle of sticks in her small arms, and Whisper was dragging a larger branch backward behind her. The wolf dropped it on the ground, tongue lolling out of her mouth, panting with her accomplishment. "That should be enough wood to last us for days!" She said cheerfully.

Kate laughed. "It would be if we had any means to cut it into smaller pieces. But I appreciate your effort!"

The wolf flopped down and huffed in feigned indignation. "Can I help it if I don't have hands?"

"Not with firewood, no. But you can try to catch us something larger than stale bread for our dinner." Kate suggested.

Whisper got to her paws and nodded.

"I'll see what I can find. I'll be back soon." With that, she dashed off into the forest.

Gwen turned to Kate with a confused look on her pleasant face. "Where's she going?"

Kate offered her a smile, "Don't worry; I asked her to try to find us something else to eat. She'll be back soon."

The little girl nodded and began feeding some of her smaller kindling into the fire. After a while, she stopped and then held her hands up to the warmth. "I wish I could understand Whisper like you do." She said.

Kate, who had been working at creating a simple lean-to against a nearby large oak tree, stopped what she was doing and came over to sit beside the fire for a moment.

"How did you learn to talk to her anyway?" Gwen asked.

"I cast a spell."

"Why can't you do that for me?" The little girl's blue eyes were accusing.

"There has to be some innate magic in you for it to take hold; I'm sorry," Kate replied.

Gwen crossed her arms in front of her chest and pouted. "I wish I was a witch."

Kate smiled, "But then no one would like you. Don't you know that all witches are evil . . . and ugly?" She was only half joking.

Gwen immediately stopped sulking and sat up straight. "Oh no, you're not evil. And I think you're beautiful!"

Kate smiled, but it was full of regret as she touched the burn scars on her face with contempt. "That's kind of you to say, but how can I be beautiful when I look like this?"

Gwen immediately crawled over to where she was sitting and took her face in her little hands. She traced the deep, craggy lines of the burns with her pale fingers. Gentle as a feather, she touched all over Kate's face. When she was done, she still held the witch's face in her hands as she said, "I've seen you, and I think you're beautiful. You help people. You're kind, and you have a good heart. You're beautiful where it really matters."

Kate's brown eyes welled with tears. "Thank you." She whispered.

Gwen patted her knee and then scooted back to her seat, smiling.

A few moments later, there was a rustling sound in the underbrush, and then Whisper trotted out, carrying a hare in her mouth. She laid it before Kate proudly and wagged her tail.

Gwen gasped in shock at the sight of the dead hare. But Whisper said, "Tell her not to worry. This one was old and sick and did not suffer when it died."

Kate translated, and Gwen's disapproval seemed to subside. "We need to eat, Gwen. Even if that sometimes means taking another's life to feed our own."

The little girl narrowed her eyes. "Why can't we just eat vegetables and trees?"

Kate smiled slightly. "Those are wonderful things to eat, but not everyone can survive on plants alone." She glanced at Whisper. "A wolf, for example, has to have meat. And Whisper says that the hare was killed quickly and did not suffer."

Gwen looked skeptical and then furrowed her eyebrows in thought. "I guess you're right; some things must die so that we can live. Even plants?"

Kate nodded. "Aye, plants die so that we may eat too. As long as something doesn't suffer before it dies, I think we have to accept that it's a natural part of life."

"All right. As long as Whisper says she didn't hurt it."

The wolf slowly shook her head from side to side, and the little girl patted her on the shoulder. "Then thank you for helping to feed us." She said.

Kate took the hare and then moved off and away from the fire in order to butcher it without Gwen seeing that grisly process, too. She called back to Whisper, "Please grab a log from the fire, if you can, and bring it over here so that I can see what I'm doing."

The wolf gingerly grabbed the end of a branch that was sticking out of the fire and pulled on it. It came free fairly easily, and she walked over to where Kate was waiting with it hanging sideways from her mouth. Whisper eyed the dancing flames on her makeshift torch warily. Kate took the offered branch and placed it on the ground across a rock, making sure the fire wouldn't spread anywhere else. Then she set to work skinning the hare for their dinner.

After a short time, Kate returned to the fireside with the hare prepared on a long stick. She had snuffed out the torch with her foot. She placed the spit over two tall sticks, which were on end on either side of the fire. "There. It won't take long as there's not a lot of meat to cook."

They all sat back and waited. Eventually, Kate deemed that the meat was ready, so she removed the spit and divvied up the contents for each of them. Whisper's stomach growled, but she pushed her portion away with her nose. "I can go find my own food. You two should eat that; it's not much for either of you." She stood up and started to walk back into the forest again.

When Gwen saw what the wolf had done, she called after her, "Thank you!"

Kate agreed, "Aye, thank you, Whisper."

The wolf was gone much longer this time, and Kate was beginning to worry about her friend. At last, she came padding back into the small clearing, licking the last remnants of blood off of her lips. She flopped down beside the fire and sighed with satisfaction.

"Your second hunt went well, I take it?" Kate asked, amused.

The wolf nodded and then promptly placed her head on her forelegs, ready to fall asleep. She glanced at Kate, and Kate thought she caught something in Whisper's hazel eyes.

Gwen didn't see the look and giggled as she moved to lie down next to the furry beast. The little girl rested her head against Whisper's middle and stretched out towards the fire. Then she pulled her little cloak around herself and closed her eyes.

Absently, the little girl trailed a hand through Whisper's fur, fiddling with the red ribbon around her neck. As she did so, Kate was certain she had caught something troubling her furry friend.

Within moments, Gwen's little hand had dropped to her side, and she was snoring softly.

Whisper had closed her eyes, but Kate thought she could see the wolf breathing rapidly as if she were under stress.

She cleared her throat, not too loudly that she would disturb Gwen, but she saw Whisper's ears flick towards the sound.

"Do you want to talk about it?" She asked quietly.

For a long moment, Whisper didn't move, and Kate was afraid the wolf had ignored her until she fell asleep. But then she opened her eyes and raised her head slowly.

"There's nothing to talk about," Whisper finally said. It was mumbled so softly, even within her mind, that Kate found herself straining forward to hear her better.

Eventually, Whisper looked down at her paws and sighed deeply. "This is not how I thought my life would turn out."

Kate waited patiently and then offered her an encouraging nod. "How did you think it would go?"

At that, Whisper laid her ears back in embarrassment. "I don't know what I really expected, but it wasn't anything to do with being a were-wolf. Whatever I was before this, I'm not now, and I don't like it." She suppressed a whimper.

"I'm a monster, and that's all anyone's ever going to see me as."

The words hung there in Kate's mind, and the witch could hardly believe that she didn't immediately respond. When she didn't answer, Whisper looked up at her and pleadingly asked, "why am I a monster?" Her voice sounded pitiful and weak.

Kate narrowed her eyes at that and shook her head fiercely. "First, you're not a monster." She held up a hand to forestall Whisper interrupting her. "Second, stop feeling sorry for yourself." She gestured at her burn scars. "You think you're the only one who has had troubles in their life? The only one who went through a horrible experience? The only one who struggles? The only one who wants peace?" She snorted derisively, which caused Gwen to shift in her sleep.

Kate continued, quieter now, "We all want the same thing out of life: to live as we so choose in an effort to find our happiness."

Whisper blinked. She was taken aback at Kate's sullen outburst. She cocked her head to the side.

"Your life hasn't turned out the way you expected. So what? Make the most of what you already have."

Kate sat back and sighed. "You have a new family now, and we don't see you as a monster because you're not. It's not what you had before, but it's not bad, is it?"

Whisper quickly shook her head.

"All you've ever done is help us. And we love you for who and what you are. Isn't that the most any of us could wish for?"

Whisper was silent for a long moment, just watching Kate as she blinked her eyes a few times. "It's all I've ever wanted: to be loved for who and what I am," she said very quietly.

At that, a few tears fell down her cheeks. Whisper wriggled out from underneath Gwen and padded towards Kate. The wolf sat down directly in front of her and nosed Kate's head up with her snout so she was looking her in the eyes.

"I'm sorry, and I know you're right; it's just I don't know what to do with my life anymore."

Kate wrapped her arms around the beast and squeezed her friend hard as her tears continued to fall into Whisper's black fur.

"You keep doing as you have, helping people when it's needed and doing the right thing. And being with your new family."

Whisper leaned into the hug, and after a few moments, she sighed, and Kate could feel the tension easing out of her.

"You're right. Thank you." Whisper thumped her tail a few times, and Kate released her.

The wolf nodded resolutely and said, "From now on, I will do anything to protect my family." She took a big breath and then said, "And I will be a good werewolf."

Kate smiled through her tears and nodded firmly.

She dabbed at her eyes with her apron and then nodded towards Gwen. "She has the right idea; we should get some rest, too, since we're all exhausted from our ordeal earlier."

Kate poked at the fire to stoke it and then laid down with her back towards the wolf.

After a few moments, she said softly, "As long as we stick together, this family can endure anything."

Whisper thumped her tail once more and then wiggled back under Gwen's still-sleeping form. The little girl had never even opened an eye. The wolf sighed, but this time, it was in contentment.

Kate smiled to herself at the sound and then drifted off to sleep herself.

TWENTY-ONE

It went like this for the next few days: the three of them would rise in the morning and break camp, and then they would walk all day long until it was dark. They would stop and rest periodically, but it was a long and tiring journey nonetheless.

It took them three whole days of walking, and Gwen was beginning to complain, as children do.

"How much farther?"

Kate stopped walking and looked up at the sun and sky. They were still heading directly east, and if she squinted, she could make out the edge of the forest. "We're nearly out of the woods. If we keep going, we should make the coast by tonight."

The little girl nodded once, firmly, and then began to walk again with renewed determination.

Whisper had stopped walking when Kate had, and she was standing stock still, listening. Something seemed off. There was no birdsong, and the forest was eerily quiet. Throughout their long walk, nothing strange happened, so everyone finally managed to relax a bit.

The wolf sniffed the air deeply and flicked her ears this way and that, listening. She couldn't pinpoint what exactly it was, but she was suddenly very uneasy. The trees themselves seemed to be holding their breath and waiting for something.

As Gwen began to walk forward again, Kate and Whisper moved to follow her. Whisper looked left and right into the trees to try to catch sight of whatever was out there, making her feel uneasy.

They walked like this for another mile, but still, nothing happened. No monster rushed out at them, and no man jumped out to attack them either: it was creepy. Whisper felt her hackles rising. She felt certain that something bad was coming for them. And yet, her senses detected nothing out of the ordinary. It was extremely disturbing.

Up ahead, the path went from green and lined with grass to a light brown color with a sandy consistency. None of them thought anything of it; they were approaching the coast after all, so they continued forward.

As they got closer, Whisper thought she saw movement in the sand itself: a ripple near an edge. When she looked again, there was nothing there. Her nerves were beginning to fray from being on edge for so long. She took a deep breath but still smelled nothing out of the ordinary.

Gwen was the first one to reach the sandy ground, and she giggled as her feet began to make squelching sounds since the sand was wet. She stopped walking and turned around to face Kate and Whisper, who were a little farther behind her. "Why's the sand so wet, this far from the seaaaaa!" The last word ended in a shrill scream as something suddenly broke the surface of the sand and grabbed for the little girl. She shrieked in fear and surprise but had the presence of mind to jump back towards more solid ground.

She whipped her head around, searching for help, and whatever was in the sand reached a long, dirty hand up out of the sandy ground, stretching for the little girl's ankles. It had extremely long fingers, and they were tipped with wickedly sharp, needlelike black claws. It grasped ahold of Gwen's foot and began to pull her towards the sand slowly. As it did so, more of the creature emerged from the quicksand.

It was humanoid in shape and appeared to be female, with long, wet and lank dark hair that pooled in the sand as if it were water. She had huge, disc-like black eyes, and they were wide and sinister-looking. The sun didn't seem to reflect in them, and it was otherworldly.

She reached her other arm up and out of the sand; it had faint black stripes on it that blended in almost invisibly with the patterns in the swirling sand when matched with her caramel-colored skin. She opened her mouth and let out a whistling shriek, and they could see several rows of prickly sharp teeth around her round-shaped and open mouth.

As the creature heaved herself forward to get a firmer hold on Gwen, Whisper caught sight of a long, fish-like tail churning in the sand. As she lurched sideways, moving within the sand as if it were water, sunlight glinted off a gold medallion hanging around her neck.

Whisper growled, low and dangerously, as the creature started to drag poor little Gwen right toward her pointed teeth.

Whisper and Kate leaped into action as the creature started pulling Gwen closer. Kate threw herself flat on the hard ground and reached out for the little girl while Whisper ran around and tried to harry the creature. The wolf barked and snarled and caused as much sound as possible to create a distraction that seemed to work at first. But then the creature quickly slashed her long claws toward Whisper's face, and the wolf yelped and jumped back in shock and pain. Blood welled, and she shook her head vigorously from side to side to try and clear her vision.

Meanwhile, Kate was trying to pull Gwen up and out of the quicksand, but the creature still had a hold of her and was slowly dragging her under. Now the little girl was up to her knees, and she was thrashing and kicking with all of her might, trying to break free, but the creature had an iron grip on her and wasn't going to let go easily. Gwen shrieked and screamed for all she was worth, though. Occasionally, the creature would let out its whistling screech again, so they were all raising quite a commotion.

Once Whisper could see again (and, luckily, the creature's claws had missed taking out her eyes), she leaped in again and renewed her attempts at focusing the creature's attention solely on herself. She would jump in close, letting her paws sink a bit in the wet sand and nip at whatever part of the creature was nearest to her. Sometimes, her teeth would connect, and she would clamp her jaws shut tight, only to be shaken off as the slippery creature writhed. She couldn't get her fangs to lock on for longer than a few moments. And her efforts did not seem to be deterring the creature from continuing to drag Gwen under.

The little girl was now up to her waist, and her weight would soon start acting against her by helping the creature to drag her down. In between her shrieks, she began to cry in fear.

Kate kept her hands locked around Gwen's arms and was still trying to pull her free. But she was losing the battle. She began to mutter under her breath. She closed her eyes and focused all of her strength on holding Gwen above the surface of the quicksand. Then, she began pouring her power and will into her words. Slowly, dark purple smoke began to flow out of her clenched hands. It flowed, like water, over to Gwen. But when it touched the surface of the quicksand, there was a fizzing sound, and the smoke began to dissipate with no effect.

"Come on, Gwen, pull!" Kate pleaded with the little girl. "My magic won't affect this creature. You've got to help me!"

Gwen's struggling had now turned into panicked spasms as the reality of her predicament began to cement itself in her young mind, as the quicksand now swallowed her waist. She was going to die. And then this creature that had a hold of her was going eat her. Hopefully, it would happen in that order.

The quicksand was now up to her shoulders, and her head would soon go under. Besides that, as she was being dragged down, she saw that Kate, who was still fighting fiercely not to lose her hold, was also being pulled towards the quicksand. Her dress was wet, and her own body was getting stuck in the sand. The little girl knew, without a doubt, that Kate would hold on to her until the bitter end. And would, in all likelihood, follow Gwen to her death.

Whisper raced around and took hold of the hem of Kate's dress in her teeth and began trying to pull them all back. The wolf hunched her back and heaved backward. On her third attempt, Kate's dress ripped, and she went sprawling onto her tail. The wolf growled and jumped forward to do it again. The creature, whatever it was, lashed her fish-like tail across the surface of the sand and grinned evilly at the wolf.

Frustrated beyond reason, Whisper threw back her head and howled long, clear and loud.

Kate did the only other thing she could think of: she prayed. She scrunched her eyes shut tight and prayed that all three of them would get out of this mess alive and intact.

Gwen could feel the quicksand slowly eating its way up her neck and into her hair. It was maddeningly snail-like about it, and she was aware of many tiny particles of sand getting stuck in her dress, on her face, in her shoes, everywhere. It was wet and cold, and the entire pit stank of dead fish and fetid water.

It was now up to her nose, and she took one last pathetic breath of air before she was pulled under completely.

She was floating, and the feel of the gritty sand against her skin was like a living thing all by itself. She squeezed Kate's hands and then suddenly lost her grip. She was now completely alone, in blackness, and was surely going to die.

TWENTY-TWO

And then, through the muck caked in her ears, Gwen thought she heard the oddest sound. Grunting and guttural growling sounds were coming toward her. There was also a loud, horrible hissing sound. She was terrified that it was the creature coming to eat her now.

Someone suddenly grabbed her wrists, and she was quickly yanked straight up. There was a popping, wet sound as quicksand was sprayed everywhere. Then she fell unceremoniously into a heap on the hard, firm ground.

She rubbed at her eyes, and once enough of the gunk was out, she opened them and found herself staring into teeth that were stained and yellowed . . . and were inches from her face. She was looking at yet another terrifying monster. She wasn't sure what she feared the most right then: the creature that had tried to pull her under the wet sand or the creature with all the teeth standing right in front of her now. And that awful hissing sound, accompanied by heavy breathing, was so close that it was making her skin crawl. The sound rumbled along and was punctuated by long, wet, grunting sounds.

"Ho boys, get back!" Called a loud and authoritative male voice.

Whatever the scaled monstrosity in front of her was, it backed up slowly on webbed feet.

When she could see something other than those nasty teeth, Gwen looked all around for Kate. "What happened?" She gasped, wiping more sand from around her mouth. "I was pulled under, and I thought I was going to die!"

Kate came over to kneel beside her and offered her a warm blanket, which she wrapped around the little girl. "He happened." Kate smiled brightly. When Gwen gave her a confused look, she jerked her head over her shoulder.

Gwen peered around her friend and saw a man standing behind two large beasts, the things with the ugly teeth. He was dressed immaculately in high white stockings and buckled shoes and had on black pants that fell to his knees. He was wearing a crisp white shirt and a red velvet frock coat edged in gold brocade that completed his outfit. He had a cutlass dangling from a sash at his waist, and he had long, curly black hair and a mustache that was curled slightly. He looked, Gwen thought secretly, rather silly.

He was bending down and scratching the scaled and scary things under their chins as if they were enormous cats. Each of them was making a rumbling, purring sound in, apparent delight.

Gwen stared at the odd sight. Then she gasped. The man was scratching his monsters with a hook in place of one of his hands!

Kate put her hand on Gwen's knee and shushed her, "It's all right, he's a friend. And he's not going to hurt the crocodiles; they're his pets." Gwen turned her confused eyes to look at Kate, "But what about his . . . ?"

Kate shook her head, "Remember that not everyone is as beautiful as you are." She touched her face, "Some of us have scars to bear from a hard or unfair life."

Gwen's eyes shone with tears, "I didn't mean . . ." She mumbled, looking at the ground.

Kate patted her knee. "It's all right, I understand. You're young yet, and we all sometimes judge too quickly."

She looked over at the strange man, "He may seem odd, but he's my friend and a good man."

Gwen nodded resolutely and then stood up on shaking wet legs. "Excuse me, sir?"

The man looked over and smiled kindly. He patted the crocodiles once more on their heads and then walked over toward them. He bowed low and took her little hand in his left and un-hooked hand. He raised it to his lips and, despite the stinky sand, kissed it gently.

"I am Captain Charles Jasper Frohmer, at your service, miss."

She giggled in delight at his formal attitude. "Please, sir, call me Gwen. All my friends do."

He smiled broadly and nodded. "Aye, aye, miss, but then you must call me Charlie. All *my* friends do." He gave a roguish wink.

Kate stood behind him and was also smiling. "You arrived just in time, too, Charlie. Thank you for saving us."

He held up his left hand and said, "Think nothing of it, Katie; I'm just glad we got here in time. If the boys hadn't been nosing around nearby, and we hadn't heard you making all of that ruckus, we might have been too late. But we heard you and came running. When we got here, that sand-tigermaid almost had you."

"What's a sand-tigermaid?" Gwen asked.

"Sort of like a mermaid, only ugly, scary, and mean as all get out. They like to lie in wait in sand traps or quicksand and then surprise unwary travelers. When we got here, she almost had you both. But the boys here tore into her 'til she left you alone."

"The . . . boys?" Gwen asked curiously.

Charlie grinned and then whistled. "Here, boys! There's a lady I'd like you to meet!"

The two crocodiles scampered over towards them, lithe and agile despite their large size, and Gwen had to stop herself from flinching away in fear. They were massive beasts, longer than she was tall and scaled and tough-looking. Their yellowed teeth poked over their jaws, and both of them had beady black eyes. They looked mean.

"This here is Port," Charlie indicated the larger and lighter, more tan-colored one. "And this here is Starboard." He indicated the smaller and darker green-colored of the two. He reached over and scratched them both under their chins. Both crocodiles stood up on their webbed toes, leaning into the gesture with pleasure.

"What . . . are they?" Gwen asked softly. She was afraid to speak too loudly lest they decide that they didn't like her and gobble her up.

Charlie proudly indicated his pets. "They are crocodiles, water beasts, and cold-blooded reptiles. They're usually not very nice, although these two sweeties were hand-raised by me from eggs. I found them when I was out sailing the local southern islands. Poor things never had a mum. But they think of me as their mum now, don't you boys?"

Each crocodile thumped his meaty tail hard on the ground.

Gwen was suddenly charmed by the strange (and fearsome-seeming) creatures. "Thank you for helping to save me. You're both very strong and terrifying creatures."

They preened under her praise.

Kate then looked around. "Has anyone seen Whisper?" There was a mild note of panic in her voice. In all of the commotion, she had completely forgotten about the wolf. After Charlie and the boys had saved them from the quicksand and sand-tigermaid, she had just been glad to be alive.

"Who's Whisper?" Charlie asked.

"She's a wolf and our friend," Gwen replied, looking towards the sides of the road.

"You two travel with a wild wolf?" His blue eyes widened in surprise.

Kate put a hand on her hip, "You have two gigantic reptiles as pets."

He had the decency to look chagrined. "Fair point, Katie."

"I'm here, Kate." Came the answer in the witch's mind a moment later. Then, the wolf walked out from among the trees. "One of that creature's hits sent me flying into a tree." She was limping and was stiff and in pain.

As she walked up to them, Charlie eyed the wolf skeptically. "And she just comes whenever you call her, just like that?" His black eyebrows were raised high and were almost into his hairline.

Kate bent down and rubbed her hands all over Whisper's fur, searching for any broken bones. "Well, yes. We look after each other. We've been friends for a while now." She straightened up again, satisfied that the wolf would heal her aches in time. "And she's not actually a wolf. She's technically a werewolf."

Charlie's eyes widened in recognition and fear, and he took a few steps back from them. Port and Starboard let out low hisses and narrowed their beady black eyes.

"It's not like that!" Gwen shouted, moving to stand between the crocodiles and the wolf.

"She's a good werewolf. She saved me. And she'd never hurt anyone. Well, not anyone who didn't try to hurt her or us first."

Charlie looked at them doubtfully. "If you say so, miss."

Kate snorted. "Oh, Charlie, please. You go around with two pet crocodiles with you everywhere you go. And they don't hurt anyone, do they?"

Charlie looked affronted. "But I raised them from eggs! Of course, they're harmless!"

Kate quirked an eyebrow. "And it's the same with Whisper. She came to me, hurt and broken, and I healed her. Now we're friends. And I know for a fact that she would not hurt anyone unless she were threatened first."

He raised his hooked hand in a placating gesture, "All right, if you say so, Katie."

She glanced at his hook. "Besides, you should know better than anyone that fearsome looks can be extremely misleading."

He sighed, "Fair point again; you win." He crouched down and offered his left hand out to the wolf. "Nice to meet you, Miss Whisper." The wolf walked towards him slowly and then sat down on the ground a few feet away. She leaned forward and sniffed but did not approach any further.

"Oh, come now, why won't you be nice?" Kate asked her.

The wolf looked up at her and then put her ears back. "They smell . . . fishy."

Charlie's eyes narrowed, "What's wrong?"

Kate laughed, "She says you three smell like fish."

He gasped and put his left hand to his heart, "My delicate sensibilities!"

Everyone laughed, and Whisper wagged her tail. The tense meeting was over, and all seemed to be well with the group again.

"If you'll all just follow us, I'll take you to some warm food and some dry beds," Charlie said. He motioned off down the trail, around the quicksand pit, and down toward the coast.

Port and Starboard began waddling off in that direction, their strange side-to-side gait interesting to follow behind. Gwen went next, still fascinated by the huge creatures. Kate walked beside Charlie with Whisper bringing up the rear.

The wolf was exhausted and found herself almost falling asleep on her paws in the growing twilight. She hoped Charlie's home wasn't far off.

She was in luck, for once they left the forest, it was only a short walk down a hill towards the sea and coast. After the putrid scent of the sand, the scent of salt and water was a refreshing and welcome change.

The wolf stopped walking and took a deep breath. It smelled wonderful, and she was happy (and lucky) to be alive. At the end of the fight with the sand-tigermaid, she had almost been pulled under herself. It had been a terrifying experience since there had been little she could do to help Kate and Gwen. The wolf shut her eyes at the memory of little Gwen sliding beneath the surface of the quagmire, with Kate holding onto her and them both kicking and screaming.

If she lost her small family now, Whisper honestly had no idea what she would do. It wasn't enough that they had lost their nice home, but now she had almost lost the two people she cared about the most as well. She whimpered softly in the back of her throat. She had already had to get used to life as a werewolf, despite not remembering living as anything else beforehand, and then she had gotten used to having someone else around who talked and listened to her.

When she found Gwen, their little family seemed to be perfect and complete. Both Kate and Gwen were all Whisper had anymore.

Charlie glanced behind himself and noticed that the wolf was no longer following them. He patted Kate on the arm and then walked back the way they had come. He found her sitting in the shadows of the trees, whimpering and looking like a lost kitten.

He knelt near her and offered his left hand. "It's alright, girl, come on." Then, he waited patiently. He was dimly aware of the rest of the group stopping and waiting behind him.

"We're just going down to my home. It'll be all right." He looked over his shoulder and then looked back and smiled at the wolf. "I can agree with you on this one; you've got a great family there. I understand you want to protect them. But I promise that I won't let anything bad happen to them either. Katie's a good friend of mine and has been for many years. I won't let anything happen to little Gwen either; she's just too pretty for words, and she seems to have a good heart. Me and my boys will protect you all."

At his words, the wolf's tail wagged slowly. She walked over towards him and then nudged his hook hand with her wet nose. He automatically used it to scratch behind her torn left ear gently. She made a small sound of pleasure, and he smiled broadly. "Seems you and me have something in common, eh?"

The wolf nodded, clearly and distinctly. Then she got up and began walking back towards the group to join them. He followed, satisfied with himself for offering an olive branch to a creature he would have, in all likelihood, despised on sight. Not everything was as it seemed at first glance.

He smiled to himself and then rejoined the group.

TWENTY-THREE

After walking a little farther, they came to the water itself. The town of Tagosta stretched parallel along its banks, and, in the growing dark, many homes had candles or lamps lit in their windows.

As they approached the road, Kate stopped walking, but Charlie continued. When he realized she was no longer beside him, he looked back. "What's the matter?"

"It's just that . . . villagers don't like us much." She had her hood drawn up to cover her face, and one of her hands was holding it up protectively.

Charlie shrugged. "Perhaps, but they hate the thought of an upset pirate even more." He grinned and then continued walking into Tagosta.

"I thought you gave that up!" Kate hurried to catch up to him.

He gave her a lopsided grin, "I gave up the *bad* part of pirating: the stealing from everyone part. Now I steal from the rich."

She snorted. "What do you do with all that treasure now? Aren't you rich enough after all those years on the high seas?"

He waggled his black eyebrows. "Of course I am; how else do you think I can afford to dress so dashingly?"

He continued, "Once I got enough to live the rest of my life comfortably with, I decided that I should help those around me, too. I always liked this port of call, so when I finally decided to make a berth, I came here. When I go out pirating, I keep a little for myself to keep up with expenses, you understand, and I give the rest to the town." He shrugged. "It's a good, solid arrangement. I donate anonymously to the town, although everyone knows it's me, of course, and the villagers look the other way when the authorities feel like hanging pirates."

Kate grinned. "You sly devil! Steal from the rich to give to the poor; you're brilliant!"

He returned her grin with one of his own, "Thank you, my dear! I learned of that way of life from a fellow I met on one of my northern routes. Robin . . . something or other, I can't remember." He waved his left hand flippantly.

Charlie kept walking, and now the group followed him. "And the villagers tend to simply look the other way when me and the boys come into town." He looked at the crocodiles fondly. "Most of them are terrified of them, naturally, but many of the children adore them."

As they began to pass buildings, several of the candles and lamps abruptly went out.

"See what I mean?" Charlie indicated them and then shrugged. "Doesn't bother us, though; we keep doing what we love and donating and living how we like. Don't we, boys?"

The crocs rumbled their approval.

"There's an inn up here called the Laughing Rat; you'll love it. They've got good hot food and fresh cold beverages, and the music is wonderful! And . . . very unique!" He started walking a bit faster, and the group had to hurry to keep up with him.

They arrived outside the inn and could hear the strains of a fast song being played inside. Drums were keeping the beat, a horn blaring out loud and strong, and a stringed instrument and singing, too, though none of them could make out the words.

The four-legged members of their party thought it best for everyone if they waited outside. So Charlie led Kate and Gwen inside to take a seat at a table in the corner of the tavern. He motioned to a barmaid, who nodded and came over to take their order.

Charlie ordered full dinners for all three of them and then sat back to watch the show.

On a small stage to the left of the bar was one of the strangest sights Kate and Gwen had ever seen. There was a raised platform so everyone in the room could have a clear view of the entertainment. And the entertainment itself was truly unique, as Charlie had promised.

An old donkey was standing by the back wall, leaning against it for support. He looked so ancient and weary that the wall seemed to be the only thing holding him up on his four hooves.

In front of him was the thinnest hound dog Kate had ever seen. The poor thing looked more than half-starved as his ribs stuck out of his skin. Sitting on the dog's back was a mangy she-cat whose white whiskers were crinkled and disheveled. She was languorously washing a front paw across her face. Sitting in front of her, on a small stool, was a pathetic rooster who looked like he was about to lose the rest of his ragged feathers. Even his red comb lacked its brilliant ruby color.

Kate glanced at Charlie in concern. "Why are these sad and sick-looking animals on a stage?"

Charlie held up his left hand, "Shhh, just watch. They're about to start again."

Gwen was sitting on the edge of her seat, looking at the animals excitedly. "Maybe when we leave, we can take them with us? They don't look so good."

"It'll be all right, just watch," Charlie said.

The three of them waited expectantly, watching the sorry-looking group on the stage.

At some unseen cue, the donkey suddenly threw back his head and brayed loudly. The room erupted into a chorus of cheers. Kate furrowed her eyebrows in confusion. "What is going on here?"

Charlie just grinned.

Then, all four animals seemed to come to life for the first time in ages. The donkey stomped his hoof in time as the dog's eyes widened with life, and he began to beat an easy rhythm on a drum with his paws. The donkey then used his long tail to strum on a lute resting on a small table behind him. They both bobbed their heads with pleasure at the sounds.

The rooster then leaned forward and began to blow into a horn that was situated on the front of his perch. He came in low and slow and matched the beat and sound of the other two instruments perfectly. The loud, clear brass notes rang out, and the tempo started to pick up. He flapped his wings excitedly. The cat nodded in time to the beat, too.

Suddenly, she straightened up and opened her mouth and began to sing. The sound that came forth from the old girl was nothing short of wonderful. She crooned in time to the sweet jazz music, winding her gravelly voice naturally into the sounds created by the others. What all four of them created was pure, magical music.

As they finished the song, with the horn ending on a long, warbling note, the tavern went crazy. Patrons stood up and clapped thunderously while other people banged their tankards on the bar and whooped in approval.

Kate found herself staring in amazement at the group. "They all seem so . . . full of life when they play! It's an amazing transformation!"

Charlie just grinned. "Aye, it's part of their act. They pretend to be all sad and miserable, but then, when they start to play, they can't hide their joy. Isn't it wonderful?"

"They're actually perfectly well cared for; they live with the innkeeper and his wife here," He added.

Kate returned his big smile and then clapped as loudly as the other patrons.

Meanwhile, Gwen was sitting and staring at the musicians. The little girl's blue eyes were wide with wonder, and she giggled in delight.

"Didn't I tell you they were fantastic?" Charlie asked.

Gwen stood up on her seat so she could see better, and then she yelled along with the rest of the tavern. "More, more!"

After a few more songs, the musicians retired from the stage. They walked off to the loud and excited noise of the crowd. And each one of them had a swagger in their step; they were obviously proud of their craft, and rightly so.

When the group was finished eating, Gwen wanted to go meet the animal musicians, so Kate took her over to the barkeep. He jerked his head behind him, and they walked around the bar into a back room.

All four animals were nose-deep in their food or water bowls. And, while they looked tired when they got closer, Kate noticed that not one of them looked miserable or unhealthy in any way. Even the dog's sickly ribs had merely been cleverly applied stage makeup.

Gwen squealed with joy and looked as if she wanted to rush towards the cat and pick her up, but she restrained herself and merely hopped from foot to foot in excitement. Like all children, the little girl loved animals.

When they heard them enter the back room, the donkey's long ears flicked over in their direction. The dog walked over and sniffed Gwen's hand and then leaned in to be petted, his long, thin tail thumping loudly on the dirt floor. The rooster flew over and landed on Kate's offered outstretched arm, and the cat sauntered over and wrapped herself around Gwen's ankles. It seemed that they were all used to entertaining their fans.

Gwen giggled in pleasure and gave the animals all the attention they asked for. After a few minutes, Kate said, "Perhaps we should go now; animals are waiting outside for us as well."

Gwen reluctantly put the cat down on the ground. "All right." Then she turned to the musicians. "If you ever want a new place to call home, I think we can find room for you. And we love all sorts of animals! We've got a wolf and two crocodiles out back right now!" She grinned and skipped over to Kate.

Kate caught the look of alarm that passed between the four animals and had to stop herself from smiling. "They're perfectly well-behaved." She winked at them, and then she took Gwen's hand and led her back to the table and Charlie.

Then, all three of them went outside. They didn't see Whisper or Port or Starboard when they first walked outside, but when Charlie whistled, they all came walking up from the beach, which was across the road from the tavern.

"My home is this way. I'm sure everyone is exhausted, so I thought we'd go to bed," Charlie said.

Kate nodded and stifled a yawn with the back of one hand. Charlie led the way down to a small harbor at the other end of the main street of Tagosta.

As they got closer to the end of the line of houses, Gwen asked sleepily, "Are we soon there? We're running out of houses. Where do you live?"

Charlie smiled, "Not in a house, actually. I live on the water."

When Gwen tilted her head to the side in confusion, he continued, "I live on a ship. She's docked in the harbor."

After a few more moments of walking, they reached the harbor, and Charlie indicated a medium-sized sloop near the end of the dock. "There she is, The Jolly Roger!" He pointed with his hand proudly.

They walked down to the ship, and Charlie held out his left hand to help Kate and Gwen onboard. Port and Starboard lumbered up the gangplank and then settled down near a small doorway towards the front of the ship. They were both asleep almost instantly.

Whisper was more cautious. The wolf walked up the gangplank and then looked around the deck. She sniffed and then eyed the ropes suspiciously. "What are all the ropes for?" She asked Kate.

Kate relayed the question to Charlie, and he gestured towards the white things bunched up along wooden poles. "All the ropes, or rigging, help to control those white things, the sails. The sails catch the wind, which makes the sloop, er, ship, move through the water. It's quite elegant. And she's small enough that I can sail her myself."

Whisper nodded once and then walked towards the opposite end of the ship as the crocodiles. She turned around three times and then settled into a pile of folded sails to sleep.

Charlie motioned for Kate to follow him. He picked up Gwen and carried her since the little girl was nearly asleep on her feet. He took them through the small door at the front of the ship, and Kate was pleased to see a modest-sized living area inside.

They all bedded down for the night, Kate and Gwen in the little bed and Charlie in a hammock, which he strung up across two hooks hanging from the ceiling. "For when the seas get too rough." He explained to Kate when she gave him a quizzical look.

Once everyone was settled, it wasn't long before the entire group was fast asleep after their exciting and frighteningly busy day.

TWENTY-FOUR

The next morning, Whisper woke to the sounds of a rooster crowing at dawn. After hearing Gwen gush about the amazing animal musicians the night before, the wolf had no doubt who the rooster was. She sighed and tried to go back to sleep. Moments later, she felt the ship beneath her quivering, followed by two loud splashes. Alarmed at the sounds, she got to her paws and looked around.

Charlie was now out on the deck and was watching something over the side in the water. When the wolf walked up to him, he smiled. "It's just Port and Starboard; they go for a swim early every morning. They'll sleep most of the day then, in the sun, of course."

Whisper tilted her head to the side. "It's all right, just an odd quirk with crocodiles. They love the water and the sun." The wolf sneezed, and Charlie nodded. "I agree, lying in the sun is nice, although doing it for too long makes one rather hot."

Gwen joined them, and the little girl couldn't hide her excitement. "Do you think we could take her out, Charlie?"

He beamed. "Of course! Once we've all had breakfast, I'll pull out her sails, and we'll go for a quick bout out onto the bay. You're going to love it!"

At the mention of breakfast, Whisper's stomach growled, and the wolf flattened her ears, looking embarrassed.

Kate's voice drifted over from the open doorway, "I heard that. And I can fix it."

She walked out carrying a tray with food on it, which she placed on a gunwale. "I've made us all some breakfast." She put a bowl down on the deck for Whisper and then motioned to Gwen and Charlie to each take food from the tray for themselves.

It was simple fare, some bread and fruits, but they all ate gratefully. When they were finished, Port and Starboard returned and came over to Charlie. Each crocodile offered him something. They then both waddled over to their sleeping places and lay down in the warm sunshine.

Charlie took their gifts and smiled broadly. "It seems that we'll be having fish for lunch!" He announced.

When everyone was ready, Charlie trimmed the sails and hauled on the rigging. He did so all by himself, with everyone else simply trying to stay out of his way.

It didn't take him long before they were soon sailing away from the dock. He took them out onto the water, controlling the tiller and easily steering them clear of the other ships. Gwen stood by the railing and gazed back toward Tagosta. She grinned as the air whipped her black hair around her head.

Kate stood beside Charlie, watching how he expertly controlled the sails and the direction they were going. "You make this look so easy."

"I've been a sailor all my life, so I've had plenty of practice." He grinned. "Would you like to try steering her?" Kate nodded enthusiastically, and he moved over to let her take the wheel (or helm, as he told her).

She turned them towards the open ocean, and as the wind picked up, they picked up speed as well.

Whisper was at the front of the ship and had her front legs dangling off the end. Her tongue was lolling out of her mouth, and she was turning her head this way and that, sniffing the salty sea air. As they started to go faster and the wind rippled through her fur, she threw back her head and howled in delight.

They sailed around the bay for several hours until the sun was riding high in the sky at noon time. Then they dropped anchor and enjoyed the fresh fish Port and Starboard had provided them with. In the afternoon, they lounged on the deck, relaxing in the warm sunshine. All in all, it was a refreshing way to spend a day after the past few days that Kate, Gwen and Whisper had had to endure.

They were sailing back to the dock as the sun was beginning to dip towards the horizon, and they were almost within sight of the Laughing Rat when Gwen, who was up the mast sitting on a little wooden seat looking all around, called down to Charlie and Kate. "I see smoke!"

Kate raised her eyebrows in alarm. "Can you make her go any faster?" She asked Charlie.

He nodded and then took to hauling on lines and sails, pushing and pulling on things until he grunted with satisfaction. A moment later, the Jolly Roger shot forward through the water, quick as an arrow. They sailed around the last bend towards the harbor and saw what had caused the smoke. The Laughing Rat was on fire!

They docked the ship as quickly as possible, and then the entire group jumped out onto the dock to see what was going on. Villagers were running back and forth; some of them were trying to grab pails of water, some of them were trying to grab things from the inn, and others were running around in a panic.

The fire wasn't completely out of control yet, but if people didn't get it reined in soon, it would destroy the entire inn and then, perhaps, move on to some of the neighboring wooden structures. Fires were extremely dangerous and could destroy entire villages if they weren't stopped in time, so many of the villagers were trying to help.

Kate pulled Gwen aside and told her, "Please go wait on the ship; you'll be safer there."

Gwen stuck her bottom lip out, pouting, "But I want to help."

Kate nodded, "I know, we all do." She glanced back towards the ship, "But someone's going to need to keep an eye on Port and Starboard. They can't help this time, and I don't think Charlie would want them to get hurt from being in the way. Can you go back to the ship and watch them, please?"

The little girl didn't seem convinced, but she nodded resolutely. "All right." She rushed back to the ship and disappeared below decks.

When she was confident Gwen would be safe, Kate turned to Whisper. "Can you find . . ." But she never got to finish because there was a roar from in front of the tavern.

"WHERE ARE THEY?!?!?"

Kate's eyes widened in shock and fear. The wolf put her ears back in distress, too. They both recognized that voice. It was Jacob Grimm, come for them yet again.

"I know they're hiding here! Give them to me, or I'll burn all of Tagosta to the ground!"

TWENTY-FIVE

"How did he find us?" Kate whispered.

Charlie looked concerned as he leaned towards her. "Friend of yours?"

"Not exactly. He's been trying to kill us for a while now, and he's almost succeeded several times, too.

"He must have come back to the cottage and searched through the ashes. Then, when he didn't find any of our bones, he must have gotten suspicious. This is the closest village, so he came here first." Kate said.

Whisper's hazel eyes narrowed, and she growled. "Let's finish this once and for all."

Kate's eyes were wide and full of fear, though. "Why can't we just run again? Cross the sea with Charlie? Just get away from him. I want us to be able to live out our lives in peace without him."

A tear trickled down her cheek. Charlie moved in and wiped it away with his left hand. "Now, now, everything will be all right."

"But he just keeps coming after us." Kate shook her head in dismay, closing her eyes.

Charlie furrowed his eyebrows. "If he hasn't taken the hint yet to leave you alone, I doubt he ever will. You have to face your problems, Katie. Don't worry, though; I'm here to help you this time. And if it comes to it, I'll fight him myself." His eyes glinted dangerously.

Whisper nodded her head firmly.

Kate heaved a sigh and then nodded as well, opening her eyes again. "Maybe you're both right. There doesn't seem to be any sense in running because he keeps finding us anyway. He will continue to torment us until he's dealt with, once and for all. Maybe it's time we took a stand . . . even if it ends up being our last one." She chuckled, but it held no hint of mirth.

Charlie grinned fiercely, "Aye, that's the spirit! If we're going down, we're going down fighting!"

He leaned in conspiratorially and said, "But take it from me; I don't think we're going anywhere." He winked at the wolf. "It's this gentleman who won't know what hit him!" He gestured contemptuously with his hooked hand towards where Jacob's voice was coming from.

Whisper's tail wagged once in agreement, and then she turned and growled towards their enemy.

"I don't know how to fight, though." Kate fretted.

Charlie said, "It's all right; I happen to be an expert swordsman."

"Aye, but he's a huntsman, so he knows all sorts of weapons as a part of his trade," Kate said.

He smirked and pointed at himself with his hook, "Pirate."

Kate giggled, and this time, it had a hint of amusement, even if it was also nervous.

"Where are you, witch?!?" Jacob thundered.

"Let's just get this over with," Kate said. She took a deep breath and then squared her shoulders before stepping off of the dock and into the street proper.

The Laughing Rat was built near the other end of the pier in order to collect as many wary travelers as possible. The group walked along the main street towards it.

When he was within their sight, they saw Jacob pacing back and forth in front of the inn. His beady black eyes were darting this way and that for any sign of movement. He largely ignored the villagers who were trying to put out the fire. They also wisely gave him a wide berth.

He looked crazed with rage, and his fists were clenching and unclenching spasmodically at his sides. He had his usual weapons attire: knives on his belt, a gun, wire and rope. Whisper could also see a gleaming silver axe; the same axe, she realized with renewed anger, which she had seen so many months ago in her Grandma's cottage.

The wolf snarled and made to leap towards him, but Kate grabbed her by her neck ruff and held her back. "Easy. We don't want to get too close to him, or he might do something to hurt an innocent person." She said.

Charlie nodded, his blue eyes locked onto the Huntsman and watching the other man's every move.

"We need to draw him out and away from here." He chanced a glance back towards his ship. "We should try to get him onto my ship, then we can sail out onto the water and away from other people." His eyes glinted maliciously, "Besides, a pirate's best asset is his ship, and if I can get him on unfamiliar footing, I should be able to beat him."

Kate's eyes widened in alarm. "But I just told Gwen she would be safe on your ship!"

Charlie made a tsking sound, never breaking his eye contact with Jacob. "She will be fine, so long as she remains below decks."

As the three of them inched slowly closer to where the Huntsman was pacing, they watched in alarm as he suddenly grabbed a nearby woman who walked too close to him. He wrapped a meaty arm around her waist and held a wicked-looking curved knife to her throat.

"Come out, come out! If you don't show yourselves now, this one is going to die, and it'll be on your heads!" He shouted, still looking around wildly.

"Jacob, that's enough." Kate's voice was barely audible, and Whisper could tell she was frightened, but she stepped out into the light of the fire and faced him without flinching.

At first, she wasn't sure the demented man had heard her, but he slowly turned towards her voice and said, "Ah, Kate! It's about time you showed up. I've been waiting for you. And I've been busy." He jerked his head behind himself, indicating the still-burning inn.

"Let her go," Kate said, more loudly this time. Her voice barely shook as she indicated the woman whose eyes were wide and panicked. Her eyes reflected the firelight.

Jacob grunted dismissively. "If I let her go, then you'll just run away again." He pulled back on the woman, and she bent backward, yelping in sudden pain and fear. Kate took an involuntary step forward and raised her hand when he did so, and he leered at her. "You can keep running, but I'm always going to find you." His eyes flicked towards Whisper. "And that monster, too."

"She's less of a monster than you are. She hasn't hurt anyone. Look what you're doing now! You're going to destroy innocent lives and an entire town just for revenge." Kate said. "You don't have to do this, Jacob, please."

He sneered and remained where he was with the woman in front of him, shielding his own body. "I think that we do. We've been doing this dance for ages, and I've grown bored with it. You're a danger to anyone near you; you're a witch, and an abomination, so you must be destroyed. It's really that simple. Since it's my job to take care of dangerous things, I get the pleasure of dealing with you. Our personal history makes my job that much more enjoyable."

His eyes slid over to Whisper, whose fur was bristling out in all directions. She looked almost twice her normal and already huge size.

"As for you, beast, I thought I'd taken care of you already." He sniffed derisively, "No matter, once I'm done with the witch, I'll cut your heart out nice and slow. It is a shame, though, as you would have made a lovely wife for me." He shot a dark glance toward Kate.

Kate's eyes narrowed, "What are you talking about?"

"You mean you don't know?" He said in mock sympathy. "You don't know the monster's story? What's the matter, you didn't think to ask?" He added scornfully.

Kate looked at Whisper, but the wolf now looked confused, tilting her head to one side with her ears laid back. "What are you talking about? I know she's actually a werewolf if that's what you mean. But I don't see how that . . ." Kate began.

But he interrupted her, "Before *it* became a monster, it was a girl: a young, human girl. She was fair enough, I suppose, although she lacked some . . . qualities like you have." Jacob leered again.

Kate's eyes narrowed. "What does that have anything to do with her being your wife?"

"I saved her from another monster. But when I came to collect my payment, either money or her as my bride, her parents denied me." He snarled the words out like it was his absolute right to possess whatever he wished.

Whisper began to growl at that. It started as a very low and quiet rumbling deep within her chest, but after Jacob finished speaking, it was a snarl that bubbled out and over her jaws, growing in volume and ferocity.

When he heard the sound, he grinned. "Ah, so you do remember then!"

He peered around the woman he was still holding, his tone now gloating, "And do you remember what happened to your parents when they denied me what I wanted and what I was owed?"

Whisper's lips peeled up from her sharp fangs, and spittle began to drip from her jaws.

"I killed them for interfering." He smiled triumphantly.

The wolf lurched forward and almost pulled Kate off of her feet, but she held on to her fur. She began to mumble softly to her friend, trying to calm her. "Easy now, easy."

Jacob continued baiting the wolf, though, "After I killed your parents, you went mad. You transformed into the creature you are now, and then you attacked me. Me! The Huntsman! Imagine!" He snorted in contempt. "Well, you *tried* to attack me at any rate. And I thought I had killed you." He narrowed his eyes in hatred. "But I was wrong. I won't make that mistake again, beast; you mark my words!"

Kate had to dig her heels in to keep Whisper from rushing forward. Charlie laid a restraining left hand on her shoulder, too. He nodded pointedly towards the wolf's eyes; they were glowing a sullen red color. Kate felt her own eyes widen in shock; if the wolf lost control now, she might very well turn around and attack her friends. Kate's grip slipped, and she lost her hold on the wolf.

Whisper took one bounding leap forward and then stopped, stock still, her tail held out stiffly behind her like a bottle brush, her fur standing on end and her eyes blazing red. Kate gasped and put a hand to her mouth at the same time; she felt certain the wolf was going to tear Jacob to pieces, yet she was restraining herself with effort, shaking as she stopped herself from continuing forward.

"Translate for me, please." Her words in Kate's mind were clipped and concise and very soft, yet conveyed an anger Kate wasn't sure she could put into actual words. She nodded and said, "Listen, Jacob.

"It's true what you say. However, you failed to mention that you've also tried to kill a lot of innocent people. And, thankfully, you've failed with all of your attempts. The little wooden boy you tried to kill, Pinolo, has been reunited with his father, Geppetto. And little Gwen is safe and sound now as well. We protect her. I may be a beast, but at least I'm not a murdering bastard who takes pleasure from the suffering of others. I've never hurt an innocent person." Growls punctuated her words, but Kate translated her words.

There was a moment's pause once Kate had finished translating, where Jacob stared at Whisper in disgust. "Is that it? Is that your threatening comeback?" He actually started to laugh. Then he threw the woman he'd been holding to the side. She stumbled and fell to the ground, but she quickly scrambled to her feet and scurried away from the group facing off in the middle of the street.

"You want to know something else, beast?" He grinned, and it had a feverish intensity.

Charlie slowly moved forward and eased Kate farther away from the wolf and the Huntsman. His eyes flicked toward the burning inn. "We need to speed this along before the whole building bursts into flames." He breathed in her ear through clenched teeth. Kate nodded ever so slightly. He spoke quietly and without moving so as not to catch the Huntsman's attention.

Jacob continued his tirade and didn't seem to notice Charlie or Kate any longer. His gaze was now locked on the wolf alone. "Do you want to know something else? I have a cure." His voice was now quieter and more reserved. The raging madman seemed to be under control for the moment.

Whisper's red gaze faltered, and her torn ear flicked in sudden doubt.

He caught the gesture and interpreted it. "That's right, I have a cure."

Now, he glanced toward Kate and Charlie. "And I'll tell you what: if your friends leave now, I'll even give it to you." He watched their shocked faces and smirked.

Whisper felt her eyes widen in complete surprise, and she felt certain they returned to their normal color as well. So there was a cure, after all!

She hesitated, though, and the Huntsman nodded several times. "That's right, you've got it. There's a price for my cure."

Whisper made a barely audible whimpering sound, but Kate saw the wolf's posture change slightly in silent longing for a solution to her problem. Now that she knew she wasn't actually a wolf and had it confirmed by the man who was responsible, Kate knew she would long for her true form again and the life she had been denied. The wolf appeared to be standing absolutely still, but Kate saw her quivering ever so slightly as memories rushed back to her at the Huntsman's words.

Charlie gently laid his left hand on Kate's shoulder, trying to offer her support. She nodded slightly in gratitude.

Jacob continued as if he hadn't noticed anything had passed between them. "I have the cure right here," He patted a small leather satchel at his waist. "With me." He grinned savagely, "I always keep it with me due to my line of work. You never know when some creature's going to get too close." He shook his head and seemed to gain a semblance of his normal, cold and calculating mind back. "I'm nothing if not cautious, beast."

Whisper waited silently and just stared at him. He seemed to enjoy the attention and baited her even longer, letting her wait as the silence stretched on.

When Kate felt sure that the wolf was going to jump forward again, he continued. "And you may have it, on my honor, if you agree to my terms."

Whisper looked over her shoulder at Kate, who nodded. "What are his terms?"

Kate relayed the message, and the Huntsman smiled. This time, though, there wasn't a hint of the madman there; it was simply the smile of a man who knew he was about to get his way and, in doing so, would seal the fate of yet another innocent person's life by bending them to his will.

"I will give the cure to you, and once you take it, you'll revert to your human form. And when you do, you will marry me."

Whisper was about to snarl a reply, but he held up his hand, forestalling a response until he was finished. "If you become my bride, as you were meant to, and as is owed to me, I will leave your friends alone." His gaze met Kate's, and she suppressed a shudder.

"Even the witch." He finished, with his eyes still on hers. He looked back at Whisper, "But then you'll be mine. To do with whatever *I* wish."

He spoke and looked as if he were telling the truth. Kate narrowed her eyes, though, as she was well aware of his tricks. He couldn't really be telling the truth to Whisper, could he? That he would honor his bargain if she agreed to his terms?

Whisper's lips peeled back from her teeth again, and she was about to snarl when he shrugged. "If you don't do as I say, I'll simply kill all of your friends and you as well. Although I'll save you for last so you can watch all of your freakish friends die slowly and painfully first. Then you'll die, secure in the knowledge that you could have saved them if you'd only done what I asked. Besides, don't you want to be human again?" He sneered, knowing she really had no choice in the matter.

While Whisper was trying to think of a way out for herself and her friends, she suddenly flashed through it all in one abrupt, shocking memory in her mind's eye. Her Grandma's death, the creature who bit her, the Huntsman's proposal and murder of her parents in front of her very eyes, her first transformation, her encounters with Kate, Pinolo, Gwen, Charlie . . . everything came crashing back in a single, painful moment of stark clarity. She staggered on her paws.

She felt her eyes widen in surprise; she now remembered everything. But most importantly, she remembered that her name was Vivie and that the Huntsman had been bullying her for a very long time. He was responsible for many of the things that had gone wrong in her life.

The Huntsman smirked, and she realized, in a detached sort of way, that he was unaware of what she had just remembered. He thought she was simply afraid now: afraid of *him*.

The wolf narrowed her eyes but otherwise did not move. Kate and Charlie could not see her face, so they were unaware of what had transpired or that she had remembered.

Kate took a single step forward before Charlie grabbed her and pulled her back against him. "Don't." He murmured.

She ignored him, shaking herself free, and then glared at the Huntsman. "Just who do you think you are? Making these demands of us? What gives you the right to try to control us?" The witch was angry now. Her fear of this man, who had tormented her for years and who was now trying to hurt her friends again, had finally reached its boiling point.

He snorted, and his gaze shifted to hers. "Because, dear lady, it's my duty. It's my job to hunt down abominations of nature and end their existence. To keep humanity safe. To keep future generations safe. From things like you!" At the last word, he pointed an accusatory finger at her.

Kate felt herself baring her teeth at him, just like Whisper had. The expression wasn't nearly as frightening on a human, but Jacob still understood its implications.

"You're right, I *am* a witch. But I'm also a healer, and I use my gifts only to help people!" She screamed, her hands balled into fists, shaking at her sides.

His eyes narrowed. "Yes, yes, that's all well and good until you decide you don't feel like helping another human being. If one of these villagers does something to make you angry? Or if they try to hurt you in some way? What can you do to those *innocent*," He snarled the word, "people then?"

Kate's brown eyes blazed, so he continued in a mocking, sing-song voice. "And how exactly did you help the baby? Using your magic killed it. And for all I know, you actually did it intentionally." His voice was abruptly calm, and his own eyes were locked on hers.

She gasped and reeled back as if he had physically slapped her. "It was an accident. It wasn't my fault." She murmured.

Jacob snorted. "Of course not, because you only *help* people, don't you?" He sneered.

Then he took a step forward and pointed his knife at her, "But you killed the baby!"

She raised her hands to her mouth in shock and tried to stifle a cry. "I did everything I could to save our baby!"

He suddenly turned his back on her and paced closer to the inn. Charlie took that moment to come up behind Kate and shake her. She shook her head to clear her mind. "Do not let him get to you!" Charlie hissed. "We've got to get him away from Tagosta! Now!"

Jacob whirled back around and caught sight of Charlie so close to Kate. "And now you have a new lover, eh?" He sized the other man up slowly and raised a black eyebrow. "Not much to look at, is he? And he seems a bit of a fop, not like a real man anyway." He thumped himself on the chest and raised his head proudly. "I gave you everything. And you murdered our baby because you're nothing but a black-hearted, evil witch!"

Kate clenched her teeth and fought back tears, but they overcame her and streaked down her cheeks anyway. "I did no such thing. It was you who tried to murder me by burning me alive." She whispered.

He shrugged, suddenly nonchalant. "It doesn't matter now, does it?" His eyes snapped back to Whisper. "I will have her now instead."

The wolf, aware now that bigger things were at play, remained frozen. She was going to see this through to the end, even if it meant sacrificing herself to this brute. However, she had a sudden idea forming in her mind. She had plenty of evidence that Jacob enjoyed taunting and baiting people or creatures before he moved in for the actual physical kill. She was also aware, no matter if he gave her the cure or not, that he would kill her in the end anyway. She had been a monster at some point, so he had to end her life no matter what form she took. He couldn't let someone like her live.

She huffed out a small breath, and Jacob's eyes narrowed as he tried to imagine what she would do next.

"Kate, translate for me again. And I have a plan. Charlie, you're with us?" She spoke to the witch's mind.

Kate whispered the last part to the pirate quietly, and he grunted very softly in assent. Kate clasped Charlie's left hand and squeezed.

"I will do as you say, Huntsman, but only if you swear on your life's blood that you will leave my friends, *all* of them, alone from this day forward. I fully realize that you intend to kill me as soon as you have me and do not plan to give me the cure at all. Even if you did give me the cure, you would continue to think of me as nothing but a monster." She sniffed derisively and waited for Kate to translate that.

When Kate was finished speaking, Jacob furrowed his eyebrows and grunted, "I smell a setup."

Whisper lowered her ears and tried to look submissive. She even whimpered a little, which added to the overall effect.

"Tell him that I will agree to go with him and do anything he says or wishes if he spares all of you." She paused and looked back at Kate, willing the woman to trust and understand her. As she held the woman's gaze, she even winked to reassure her.

"In return for my complete cooperation, I have one final request."

Kate eyed the wolf suspiciously but nodded and then translated.

"I would have one final ride on Charlie's ship."

Jacob listened and then scratched his beard in thought. He tilted his head, thinking, but could not seem to discover anything about the request that would mean a trick. He slowly nodded. "Very well, but I will go with you in case you have second thoughts or think to escape from me again." He paused before asking, honest curiosity in his gruff voice, "Why would this mean so much to you?"

Whisper lowered herself to the ground in a completely obedient pose, just like a well-trained dog.

"Because I enjoy the wild smell of the open sea. And I want to see the sunset shining on the water. If I am to lose my freedom, I want to feel free one last time."

Kate translated and then squeezed Charlie's hand again hard. He squeezed back. They both knew what the wolf's plan was and would be ready to put it into action.

The Huntsman shrugged and suddenly relaxed a bit now that he was no longer seething with rage. He kept his hand on his knife but leaned against a barrel nonchalantly. "Well then, lead on, beast."

The wolf nodded meekly and began walking towards the Jolly Roger with her tail between her legs, looking utterly defeated and resigned. Jacob seemed to believe her posturing was genuine as he followed her while Kate and Charlie brought up the rear.

When they approached the gangplank, though, Jacob turned around and pointed his knife at Kate and Charlie. "Not you two, just us."

Charlie raised his left hand in a placating gesture and then motioned towards the sails and rigging. "She can't sail herself, sir."

Jacob muttered something vulgar under his breath about sailors and their ships but jerked his head towards the deck. "Fine, but don't try anything."

Charlie said nothing and moved to secure their departure. As he did so, he cast unhappy glances towards Jacob. The other man noticed and just returned the looks with a self-satisfied smile.

Meanwhile, Kate helped Charlie as best as she could and otherwise tried to stay as far away from Jacob as possible.

It didn't take long for Charlie to set up the rigging and to trim the sails, so, with the Laughing Rat now smoldering on the shore, they set out into the bay. Whisper, as per her plan, positioned herself along the nearest railing and hung her paws over it. She tilted her head back and closed her eyes to slits. Then she opened her mouth and let her tongue loll out as the ship began to pick up speed.

"Animals: foul and rotten barbaric creatures," Jacob muttered as he sniffed derisively.

"You might as well enjoy it too; the sea is in a fine mood today." Charlie offered.

"And what happens when the sea isn't in such a pleasant mood? We all drown then, eh? Seems like too fickle a mistress for me, bah." The Huntsman replied. It seemed that his prize won or not, he was just a miserable human being.

Charlie shrugged and steered the ship farther away from land.

TWENTY-SIX

Once they were well out into the bay, with the shore nothing but a speck behind them and only open water in front of them, Jacob realized his mistake.

"It's time, stay out of the way," Charlie whispered to Kate. She nodded and backed up towards the door that led below decks. She placed herself there to protect Gwen, who was waiting excitedly on the other side. The little girl stuck her fingers under the door and wiggled them at Kate. The witch pulled on them gently and then said, "Shhh, stay quiet, please."

Jacob appeared to be enjoying himself despite his usually wretched demeanor. He was, however, oblivious to the group's actions as his eyes were scanning the horizon and watching the bubbles around the prow of the ship.

As Charlie secured the tiller and the ship coasted forward slowly and gently, he retrieved a cutlass that had been hanging just out of sight below the helm. Unsheathing it casually, he took a few easy steps towards Jacob.

At the sound of the weapon being drawn, the Huntsman whirled around with his weapon up. He had drawn his gun swiftly and efficiently, like any trained killer. He leveled his gun at Charlie and aimed quickly. He was about to fire off a shot when Whisper unexpectedly rammed her shoulder hard into Jacob's knees. He wobbled on his feet, and the shot went wide. He struck the wolf across her nose with the butt of the gun, and she yelped. But before he could stab at her with the knife that had suddenly appeared in his other hand, she leaped away from him.

She bared her teeth and snarled. He didn't need any translation to know that he was now in serious trouble: the tables had been turned against him since he was now all alone on a small ship surrounded by three enemies who all had serious scores to settle with him.

Unfortunately for him, his gun only had a single shot primed, so he threw the weapon away and reached for another; this time, his silver axe that was also strapped to his belt. He crossed the axe and the knife in front of himself and bared his teeth. "Come on then!"

Charlie smiled sardonically and waited. "I've got all day. Why don't you give it a try yourself? Although I should warn you, if you kill us all, you'll still be stranded out here all by yourself. She won't sail for just anyone, you know."

"I could just hurt you, pirate, and then make you sail me back." Jacob spat.

Charlie winked at Kate and pretended to look offended. "Pirate? Me? Never! You insult my honor, sir!"

Jacob snorted and began to advance slowly, although he kept an eye on where Whisper was because he feared that the wolf would attack his unprotected back if she got half the chance.

He was right, of course, and she saw what he was doing and what he expected, so instead, she slunk over to where Kate was crouching. She bent down and sniffed under the door: Gwen was safe. And there were two claustrophobic crocodiles behind the door waiting with her.

Whisper nodded once in approval and then spoke to Kate. Kate's mouth set in a line of fierce determination, and she nodded. "Only when I tell you," the wolf cautioned.

She made a woofing sound under the door. A moment later, there was an answering hiss from each of the crocodiles and the sound of Gwen moving away from the door.

Whisper twitched her tail once in satisfaction and then went back to circling Jacob opposite Charlie.

She growled, and Jacob glanced at her. As he took his eyes off of his human opponent, Charlie took those mere seconds of an opportunity to surge forward in a graceful lunge that closed the distance between the two men. Jacob had no choice but to bring up his axe and knife and parry Charlie's rapid cutlass attacks. Metal clanged on metal as both men kept time with the other, their footwork creating a delicate dance of light steps as they moved across the deck.

They each had their work cut out for them; Jacob was a bear of a man and strong compared to Charlie, but the smaller man was lighter and quicker on his feet. The pirate was whip-fast, like a snake, and he ducked and weaved with natural grace. After a few moments of intense combat, Jacob was gasping for breath, although he was still easily blocking all of Charlie's attacks.

Charlie took this all into account, and when Jacob stumbled once on some rope cluttering the small deck, the pirate quickly switched to using his hooked hand as a weapon instead of his cutlass. This allowed him to move closer to Jacob, which prevented the bigger man from taking larger swings with his weapons. Without the momentum behind his powerful swings, he was reduced to having to use short stabs and quick blocks instead.

None of the closer combat styles of fighting seemed to come naturally to the Huntsman, as he was a man who usually took his kills from a distance with a gun. His close combat ability could not match Charlie's.

Since he was a pirate by trade, Charlie was more than used to fighting in close quarters, and being on the deck of a ship didn't bother him either as he placed his feet carefully without even looking down. He never once lost his footing, not even for a moment. He was also extremely proficient with his blade, whereas the Huntsman was more adept at using a gun.

They traded blows, this way and that, all across the deck while Whisper kept pace with them by always placing herself between Jacob and Kate. She knew that, if given the slightest chance, he would try to use Kate as a hostage or even kill her outright out of sheer ruthlessness. However, he seemed completely unaware of anything now other than Charlie and Charlie's blade and hook.

The pirate was now alternating between parrying with his cutlass and slashing with his hook. Once, he came within a hairsbreadth of Jacob's midsection. In doing so, he managed to rip the leather belt at his waist, which sent Jacob's remaining weapons crashing to the deck. The Huntsman had to quickly move away from them, though, because the wolf came in, snapping low at him, when he tried to reach for his belt.

He snarled incoherently at both of them in rage. As he turned back to renew his attack against Charlie, Whisper darted in and snapped her jaws shut on Jacob's left ankle. There was an audible cracking sound, and he screamed in pain and faltered. Her sharp teeth and powerful jaws had easily snapped his ankle.

"Nooooo! You stupid beast! Now you'll infect me!" He slashed drunkenly toward her, but she had already dashed away, easily out of his reach. She coughed, and it sounded suspiciously like laughter. This only seemed to enrage the Huntsman further, and he lurched towards the wolf, snarling obscenities and waving his axe and knife towards her wildly. Despite his broken ankle, he still managed to shamble around, although he was much slower now, and it was only a matter of time before he would succumb to the injury and collapse. Wobbling around on his injured leg would soon cause the ankle to stop supporting his weight altogether, and he would fall. All they had to do was stay out of his reach and wait for him to collapse.

Whisper managed to stay far enough out of his way, but they were all on a small ship and space was limited. Without watching behind herself, Whisper backed over a piece of tackle and unexpectedly tripped. She went down, and Jacob grinned viciously as he raised his silver axe over her to deliver a killing strike.

Before he could bring it down, though, Charlie lunged forward and drove his hook into Jacob's unprotected shoulder. He had meant to drag it down toward the other man's heart, but as soon as he felt the pain, Jacob spun around, dragging Charlie off of his feet, his hook still stuck in Jacob's back. Jacob wrenched the hook from his back in the same motion as he drove his axe blade up and into Charlie's stomach.

Charlie's blue eyes widened in sudden shock, and he stumbled to the deck, clutching at his midsection. He was bent over on his knees, with his head bowed, as Jacob stood over him with his axe now raised above the other man. He was just about to bring it down and behead the pirate when Whisper let out an ear-piercing howl. The sound was sharp, and it echoed across the still water.

"NOW!!!"

At her cue, Kate threw open the latch to the door that led below, and Port and Starboard rushed out onto the deck. Both of the crocodiles looked around wildly for a moment, and then both of them oriented on the sight of their master, kneeling on the deck, wounded and in pain.

Their beady little eyes narrowed, and their pointed noses quivered as they each inhaled the scent of blood in the air. Hissing ferociously, they made a mad dash across the deck directly towards Jacob.

The Huntsman's eyes widened in sudden panic and confusion: he had never seen crocodiles before, and the two coming towards him looked like monsters out of his nightmares. The scent of Charlie's blood maddened them, and they came towards him at full speed.

Jacob screeched in pain and sudden fear and jumped backward away from them. His broken ankle buckled under the strain, so he hopped on his other foot and managed to keep just out of the reach of their first strike.

He scuttled sideways like a crab across lines and cloth, trying to put as much distance between himself and the brutes as he could. But they were on a small ship, so he eventually had nowhere else to go.

Jacob now found himself backed up against the Jolly Roger's prow, effectively cornered. He glanced over his shoulder and saw the water below, clear and glossy. Port and Starboard were now advancing more slowly, hissing low and dangerously as they crept closer. As they walked together, side by side, he realized that he could not dodge around them to another part of the ship. His ankle was throbbing mercilessly, and he felt woozy from the loss of blood in his shoulder. He was trapped.

He brandished his axe before him since he had lost his knife in the struggle and used it to try to frighten them away. But they just kept coming, their piercing black eyes narrowed in hatred at him hurting their master.

"Call them off! Call your pet monsters off! You win!" Jacob screamed, his voice high and reedy in near-hysteria.

Charlie, with his head still bowed, wheezed out a breath between clenched teeth. "Can't. They don't work for me."

"What?!?" Jacob's eyes were now white around the edges as he reflexively took a step out onto the actual bowsprit of the ship.

"I cannot control them; they're simply my friends. They do as *they* wish." He looked up through his dark curls and grinned fiendishly. "Perhaps you should have chosen your friends more wisely."

Jacob continued to edge away from the pair of crocodiles slowly. Suddenly, his broken ankle gave out completely, and the loss of his balance, coupled with nothing near him to grab onto, left him floundering in midair. His arms spun wildly as he tried to catch himself, but there was simply nothing but air around him, so he fell overboard.

There was a loud splash, and then, faster than would seem possible, both crocodiles dove over the side and into the water as well.

Jacob screamed once, loud and long and still so full of hatred, and then there was nothing but the sound of receding bubbles.

Whisper didn't trust herself to look over the side, so she clenched her eyes shut tight and shuddered.

Charlie gasped for breath and then sagged onto his back on the deck. He was bleeding, and it didn't look good. Whisper whimpered, and then Kate was there at his side. She grasped his left hand and squeezed, and his eyes fluttered open. "You're all safe?" He asked quietly. She nodded as tears began to form in her eyes.

"Thanks to you, aye."

He closed his eyes and smiled.

"I . . . cannot heal you, Charlie; I don't have any of my ingredients for my potions here." Her tears began to fall, and some of them splashed onto his cheeks, too.

"It's all right. At least I won't die as a pirate but as a hero, eh?" He tried to chuckle but coughed and then grimaced in pain.

"Oh no, Charlie!" Gwen had snuck out on deck when the crocodiles had gone after the Huntsman. She now rushed to her friend's side, and her eyes widened in horror at his wounds.

"Please don't die, Charlie!"

He offered her a charming smile. "There, there, it's all right. Don't be sad for me. I get to die in battle, and that's all a pirate can hope for." He tried to wink, but his eyes stayed closed this time.

"But you and Kate were going to be my new Mama and Papa. We need you." The little girl began to cry softly.

He coughed again, weaker this time, "Hold on a moment, what?"

Kate smiled in regret and patted his shoulder. "She wanted us to be a family."

Charlie managed to nod a little. "Ah, I see now. Well, I'm sorry, miss, but there's nothing I can do . . ." He sighed, and his entire body shuddered. "I'm so tired now."

Kate cradled his head and moved it into her lap. Gwen then hunched over him and sobbed harder.

As her tears began to fall onto his wound, Kate suddenly gasped in surprise. Where the little girl's tears fell, they healed him.

In a few moments of silence, save for Gwen crying, Kate watched in wonder as Charlie's wound healed and he became whole again. He took a deep breath and then sat up slowly, gingerly touching his stomach where his wound had been. Gwen leaned back and smiled through her tears. She sniffled, and Kate handed her a cloth to wipe her eyes.

"How . . . how did you do that?" Charlie stared at the little girl in stunned admiration.

"My tears heal my friends." She stated and then blushed.

Charlie took one of her small hands in his hand. He lifted it to his mouth and kissed her hand. "My dear, *you* are a hero. Thank you."

Her blush deepened, and she looked away in embarrassment.

Charlie then glanced shyly at Kate. She, meanwhile, was staring intently at the main mast and was avoiding his gaze. "As for you, is what she says true? Do you want to be part of a family with me?"

Kate's soft brown eyes looked at him, and she smiled. "Aye, I would like that very much. And I think it's something I've been searching for a long, long time."

He got to his feet and noticed that, while healed, he still felt exhausted and shaky in his boots. He took stock of himself and nodded in satisfaction. Then, he whistled. Within a few moments, Port and Starboard had clambered back on deck, and they settled themselves on the part of the deck away from everyone else, content to sun themselves with the remaining strands of daylight.

Charlie smiled and then offered his left hand to Kate. She took it, and he pulled her in close. They stared into each other's eyes for a long moment, and then they kissed.

Gwen stuck out her tongue and looked away while Whisper wagged her tail.

When they broke apart, they both blushed and looked away from each other. Charlie trailed a gentle finger across Kate's burn scars. "I've always thought you were beautiful, Katie."

She grinned and grabbed at his hook playfully. "And I've always thought this was rather dashing."

He rolled his eyes and said, "Perhaps not dashing so much as a wonderful way to catch fish." He paused as if considering something before continuing, "At any rate, you'll know I am a good provider!"

They all laughed, and then Charlie moved away to tie off some lines. "Let's head towards shore. I think we could all use a hot, fresh meal now."

TWENTY-SEVEN

Whisper slowly walked over to where Kate was standing. The wolf's ears sagged, and she held her tail low. She looked dejected.

"I remembered everything." She said softly.

Kate knelt and wrapped her arms around the wolf, hugging her tightly. "I'm so sorry."

She heaved a sigh and leaned against the witch for comfort. "Everything from my Grandma fighting the werewolf to Jacob murdering my parents right in front of me. When he killed my parents, I got so angry that it caused me to go through the transformation into a wolf."

She whined and tucked her tail between her legs.

"He said he had a cure . . . but I didn't believe him. And now I'll never know." She cast a forlorn glance overboard toward the sea, where Jacob had finally disappeared.

"What is your name?" Kate asked her gently.

Whisper remained silent for a long time. She closed her eyes before taking a steadying, deep breath. "My name is Vivie, and I live on the edge of the forest."

Kate petted her and scratched at her ears. "I think I might be able to help you still. Wait here." She released the wolf and walked over to where Jacob's belt had been lying. She picked it up gingerly as if afraid it was poisonous. Then she opened a few pouches and satchels. Finally, she found whatever it was she was looking for because she pulled her hand away and grinned fiercely in triumph. "Aha!" She crowed.

Whisper tilted her head and flicked an ear in confusion. "What is it?"

"Come over here, please, Vivie," Kate said, kneeling once more.

At the sound of her human name, the wolf lowered her head and slowly walked over to her friend.

"I don't think he was lying." She opened her palm and showed the wolf what she had found. It was a small, glass, cylindrical vial, and it was filled with swirling bright green liquid. The liquid moved as if it had a life of its own. Kate pulled off the stopper and sniffed cautiously at the vial's contents.

"It smells like peppermint and pine needles." She rummaged through the rest of the satchels and pouches. "There doesn't appear to be anything else here that could be it."

She held it out to the wolf. "Try it."

Whisper was suddenly skeptical, and she lowered her ears. "What if it's really poison? Or what if it changes me into something . . . worse?" Her eyes were fearful, and, despite being a wolf, she seemed suddenly very young.

Kate patted her shoulder, "Things that are meant to cause harm never smell pleasant, trust me. If it were meant to be evil, it would smell foul." She held it out again, and this time, Whisper stuck out her long tongue.

Kate poured the contents onto the wolf's tongue, and then she swallowed. She shivered and then flicked her tongue over her teeth, licking her lips. "It makes my mouth itch."

Kate tried to stop herself from chuckling. "It's tingling from the peppermint."

Whisper sneezed violently and then shook her head. "It's burning my mouth!"

Kate nodded. "Relax, it will take a few moments to start working." She moved away to give Whisper some room and some privacy.

"It's starting to make me feel warm all over!" Whisper reported. She then slunk over behind the helm and out of the line of sight of everyone.

What happened next, Vivie would describe later, was confusing and a bit scary. The warm feeling spread throughout her body, starting from the tips of her paws and claws and radiating up into her legs and through her body to her head, ears and tail tip. The warmth intensified until she felt too hot and began to pant.

In a sudden release of pressure, she felt her bones popping and reforming. It wasn't painful, per se, but it was a bit uncomfortable at first. When she took a deep breath to try to relax, it seemed to help, and the discomfort faded.

Then, she felt as if her fur were sliding off of her body. She noticed, in a detached sort of way, that her tail had disappeared and that she only now had fur, or hair, on the top of her head and that it was long and honey-colored instead of black like her fur had been.

She opened her eyes (she hadn't realized she had squeezed them shut tight) and realized that she was crouching on the deck. She was, amazingly, human again.

And stark naked. Blushing furiously, she called out to Kate. "Um . . . it worked." Her voice croaked from disuse, but she could speak again out loud instead of mind-to-mind with just Kate.

Kate, Charlie and Gwen all made sounds of delight.

"But could someone get me a cloak, please? It's cold out here without any fur!"

They all laughed as Kate went to fetch her blue cloak.

By the time they all arrived back in port, the sun had set, and it was getting on into full darkness. As they tied the Jolly Roger fast onto the dock, Kate saw that the Laughing Rat was still, luckily, standing.

She pointed, and the others all looked. "It seems as if the villagers rallied and saved the inn after all."

Charlie nodded and took her hand in his. "Aye. Lucky thing, too, as I'm starving!"

They all walked down the gangplank and towards the inn.

"Dinner is on me, my treat," Charlie said.

Kate nudged him teasingly with her shoulder. "Of course it is; the town owes you again now, don't they?"

He waggled his eyebrows but said nothing.

Gwen skipped up beside them and asked, "Do you think the animal musicians are playing tonight?"

Kate wrinkled her brow. "With the fire, I'm not sure. I'd be surprised if they will be selling food tonight."

Charlie kept walking, leading the group and shrugged. "It's a business; they'll want to repair the damages, so they will be open to gather customers. They're open all the time, after all."

He then winked at them. "And perhaps they'll get a large, mysterious donation soon, too."

Gwen grinned. "Every little bit helps!"

He nodded sagely, "Aye, that it does. Come on!"

When they reached the inn, the group paused. Charlie was about to enter, but he hesitated when Kate pulled him back. She nodded towards their newest member, a young girl who appeared to be about seventeen years old with a long braid hanging over one shoulder. Her hazel eyes were questioning, and she seemed slightly bewildered. She fiddled with a red ribbon around her neck and pulled her long cloak tighter around her shoulders.

"I'll wait out here?" She asked quietly.

Kate snorted, "Absolutely not!" When the girl looked up in surprise, Kate grinned and grabbed her hand. "If saving the town won't get you food here, I'm not sure what will!"

She still looked uncertain. "But . . . I'm a . . ."

Kate shushed her. "There's no law about anyone going inside. Besides, you're on two legs now, not four. Remember that you're human again." She winked, and finally, the girl smiled. It lit up her entire face.

The four humans entered the tavern for their well-earned meal while the two crocodiles moved along to wait out back.

EPILOGUE

It was several days later when the group was sitting on the deck of the Jolly Roger out on the bay, enjoying the warm sunshine. Charlie was sitting in the shade behind the helm, gently guiding the ship where he wanted her to go. His arm was wrapped leisurely around Kate, and she was leaning against him comfortably.

Gwen was playing a game with Port and Starboard; one crocodile would go below decks while Gwen and the other one would try to hide. It wasn't working very well because the crocodiles were using their noses to cheat. However, every time one of them found Gwen, the little girl squealed with delight. Then, all three of them would scamper around the deck, with Gwen laughing and shouting in fun.

Meanwhile, Vivie was up in the rigging, sitting on a wooden seat attached to the main mast. She was gazing lazily towards the horizon, and her eyes were fluttering shut in sleepiness from the warm sun.

All of a sudden, in her mind's eye, she was in her wolf form again. But she was also staring back at her human self. How could she be in two forms at once? In her vision, the wolf bent down and wiggled her back end in the air, wagging her tail. She was happy. Vivie felt the girl, herself, furrow her eyebrows in confusion. Then the wolf came towards the girl and tugged on her sleeve, urging the girl forward. As she took a slow step forward, the girl bumped into the wolf. As soon as they touched, skin-to-fur, the two forms merged into one.

Vivie woke with a sudden start and grabbed onto the mast to steady herself. "I wonder what that was all about?" She said to herself.

She slowly worked her way down to the deck and went over to Kate. She whispered in her ear, telling her about her dream, and the other woman tilted her head, considering.

"It could mean anything. But maybe you're not done as a wolf yet?" Kate offered.

Vivie tilted her head and looked at the witch dubiously. "How could I have two forms, though?"

Kate shrugged and then stretched. "Perhaps between the curse and the cure, you can now take both forms: girl *and* wolf."

Vivie looked a little shaken, and she still seemed confused. "But why would I want to be both?"

Kate smiled kindly. "You did do a lot of good as a wolf, you know. Maybe you could do more good things?" The girl considered this and then pursed her lips in thought.

Kate stood up, and they both walked towards the prow of the ship. After a few moments of silence, as they both looked out to sea, Kate suggested, "You could always try."

"Try what?"

"Shifting forms. Go to wolf and back to girl again." Kate said.

Vivie crossed her arms in front of herself, "But what if . . . what if I get stuck?"

Kate laid a hand on her shoulder, "If you get stuck, relax and simply reverse the process." She looked into the girl's questioning eyes. "I think you'll be fine. But you won't know unless you try it."

Vivie took a deep breath and squared her shoulders. "All right, I'll try it. It's not like I wasn't used to being a wolf anyway."

She walked behind a pile of sails that needed to be mended and crouched down. She was just about to start concentrating on what she remembered it felt like being a wolf when she remembered her clothing. Wolves didn't wear dresses! So she carefully took her dress and apron off and folded them neatly on the deck. Then she crouched and tried to ignore the feel of the sea air on her bare skin. Her skin prickled at the slight breeze.

She closed her eyes and took several deep, calming breaths. Then she focused on what it had felt like being a wolf. The feel of her paws with claws scraping on the wood of the ship's deck; her fur bristling all over her body, soft and warm; her pointed ears that could detect sounds from every direction; her strong sense of smell from her wet nose; and her long, fluffy tail.

She opened her eyes slowly and found herself staring down at her paws again. She was a wolf once more!

She barked excitedly, and Kate hurried around to see her. The witch grinned and then nodded. Vivie nodded back and then reversed the process, only this time focusing on how her human body felt. Within a few moments, she was standing, stark naked, as a young girl again.

"I did it!" She cried.

Kate quickly wrapped her cloak around Vivie, and she smiled gratefully.

"I don't know what this means yet, but I'm sure it will be useful," Kate said.

Vivie hugged herself and then laughed out loud. "I don't know either, but whatever it means, I'm sure there will be plenty more adventures in store!"

Vivie linked her arm with Kate's, and the two ladies walked over to join Charlie as he stood up and stretched. He was gazing fondly at Gwen as the little girl romped around with Port and Starboard.

"There are certainly worse ways to spend an afternoon." He smiled when he saw the two of them.

Kate nodded, "Aye. And now we know that we can weather any storm as long as we're together."

Gwen giggled as she came over to them, breathless from playing. Vivie just smiled as she wrapped her other arm around the little girl. "Aye, that we can. That we can."

And they all lived happily ever after.

ACKNOWLEDGMENTS

I want to take this opportunity to thank a few key people who helped me get this project into this final format.

First, to my husband, Andy, who encouraged me to keep going when NaNoWriMo got tough and the words stopped flowing. You believed I could finish, and I did in record time, too.

Secondly, to my first editor and technical advisor, Franc, who cleaned up my messy thoughts and put them into a presentable format. This looks as good as it does because of you.

Thirdly, to my new writer friends at Sunbury Press: you took a chance on me and have started me down the path to achieving my author dreams.

Finally, to my parents, Mom and Dad, you've always believed in me. Your love and support throughout my entire life have helped me get where I am today. You taught me that inspiration and creativity are important and that I could be and do anything.

ABOUT THE AUTHOR

I'm author Eli Sickler and my love of stories started out with stories being read to me as a child. I've been an avid reader ever since I first picked up a book. My favorite genres to read are science fiction, fantasy and mythology.

Now I want to share my own original stories with the world. I like to write in the fantasy genre, creating my own worlds with magic and interesting, strong female characters.

I've participated in the annual National Novel Writing Month (NaNoWriMo) event several times. NaNoWriMo aims for writers to write 50,000 words, or more, in 30 days or less during November. I won for the first time in 2015 with my novel *House of Red*. I won again in 2017 with *Bonita Blue*. My third win with NaNoWriMo came in 2018 with *Wicked Wolves*, the sequel to *House of Red*.

I write in my spare time, along with juggling a myriad of hobbies that range from tabletop D&D games with friends, to binge-watching Doctor Who, to traveling the world. I am an avid scuba diver, animal lover, and movie nerd.

I live in central PA with my husband and three kitties.

www.ingramcontent.com/pod-product-compliance
Lightning Source LLC
Chambersburg PA
CBHW030530020726
47494CB00004B/1293